MISSION TO VENUS

Other titles in this series of

MAKE YOUR OWN ADVENTURE WITH DOCTOR WHO

Search for the Doctor
Crisis in Space
Race Against Time
The Garden of Evil
Invasion of the Ormazoids

by William Emms

This first world edition published in Great Britain 1986 by
SEVERN HOUSE PUBLISHERS LTD of
4 Brook Street, London W1Y 1AA

By arrangement with the British Broadcasting Corporation

With acknowledgement to Colin Baker as the Doctor
and Nicola Bryant as Peri

British Library Cataloguing in Publication Data

Emms, William
Mission to Venus –
(Make your own adventure with Doctor Who)
1. Games – Juvenile literature
2. Adventure and adventurers – Juvenile literature
I. Title II. Bennett, Gail III. Series
793'.9 GV1203

ISBN 0 7278 2122 9

Phototypeset by The Word Factory, Rawtenstall, Lancs
Printed and bound in Great Britain by
Anchor Brendon Ltd, Tiptree, Essex

1

You materialized with a dreadful crash. It hurled you all to the floor and there was the sound of shattering glass as gauges and crockery surrendered to the inevitable. You sat up and rubbed your throbbing elbow, looking questioningly at the Doctor. 'What did we hit this time?'

'This time?' The Doctor gave you a cold stare. 'It doesn't happen all that often, you know.'

'Too often for me,' Peri said, tenderly touching her dark head where it had connected too violently with some unmoving object.

The Doctor rose slowly to his feet, as did you. 'These minor difficulties are to be expected,' he said. 'Every time we materialize, something is displaced. It's quite simply the proposition of the object in the bath-water. Drop it in and the water rises.'

'And what, I wonder, did we drop into?' Peri wondered as she wincingly stood up.

The Doctor was studying the control console. 'A good question,' he murmured. 'At least we've arrived.'

A gauge caught your eye. It alone, among all the others, registered something. 'What does that indicate?' you asked.

The Doctor followed your gaze and was interested. 'That, believe it or not, says we're still moving.'

'And the other instruments?'

'Say we're not.'

'Oh, that's great,' Peri said. 'We materialize and immediately we've got a contradiction in terms.'

'Not necessarily,' the Doctor said, rapping his knuckle against the gauge, which remained in firm indication of what it had before. 'But it doesn't seem right, just the same.'

You crossed to a viewing-port and looked out. Nothing identifiable greeted you. Something out there was reflective because you could see a distorted image of the TARDIS, but what it could be remained a mystery. There was some movement too, but that was vague and unidentifiable.

Peri joined you. 'Anything?'

'Nothing that makes any sense.'

She also looked out. 'What am I looking at – some sort of mirror?'

'Search me.' You turned back to the Doctor, who was still peering at the gauge in some bafflement. 'Have you worked it out yet, Doctor?'

'Afraid not not.' He straightened looking remarkably cheerful under the circumstances. 'As Peri said, we have a contradiction here. And there's only one way to answer it: go outside and take a look.'

'That could be ice out there,' you cautioned. 'We don't want to freeze to death.'

'Ice doesn't often reflect,' Peri said. 'Its structure is crystalline.'

'Quite.' The Doctor moved towards the door. 'We'll find out.'

The TARDIS door moaned open and, to your relief, what came in was not freezing air. On the contrary, it was warm, rather moist and carried a certain sickly sweetness, as of rotting vegetation. You and your companions ventured out, to find yourselves in dim but definitely artificial lighting. The roof, high above, was of metal, as were the walls and the floor. Rivets and studs lined the seams and patterned the entire area. But what really took your eye were the glass jars. There were rows and rows of them, lined like soldiers from one wall to another, gleaming and obviously regularly cared for. All were joined into one by conduits at floor-level.

Inside the jars was what made Peri catch her breath. You supposed they were plants, but what sort was beyond your imagining. They reached to the very tops of the jars and, since their containers were some three metres high, they were towering and strangely manacing. In appearance they were as sickly as the odour that surrounded them, their trunks roughly half a metre thick but confused by the tendrils as thick as a man's arm that sprouted from them and tapered into tips like those of an octopus. Their colour was as bad, a weird yellowy pink, with a hint of bilious green in there somewhere. There was no avoiding the fact that they were truly revolting. The very sight of them made your stomach turn. If they were plants, what they could produce was totally beyond you. It was nothing you would care to sample, and it seemed unlikely that they developed into anything floral or beautiful. By and large, you would rather not have seen them.

Peri was studying them with scientific interest. 'I've never seen anything like this before. Have you, Doctor?'

But the Doctor's attention was elsewhere. He had crossed to the side and was examining the metal surroundings. He fished a screwdriver from the pocket of his jacket and scratched a moment. Then he stood back with a satisfied smile. 'Well, that solves the problem of why the TARDIS insisted we were still moving.' You and Peri looked a query at him and he grinned. 'We're in a spaceship.'

You were astonished. 'You mean we're somewhere in Outer Space?'

'Precisely.'

'Then can we get out of it?' Peri asked. 'I don't like the idea of being stuck with these things for long!'

'Ah, those.' The Doctor approached one of the jars and tapped on it experimentally. You were horrified to see that the tendrils immediately turned and reached blindly towards him, yearning for him and dabbing frustratedly against the glass wall surrounding them. You could not know their purpose but you certainly knew what it looked like.

'Careful, Doctor,' you warned. 'They don't look all that friendly.'

'I'm quite safe,' he said. 'They aren't trapped in these containers for nothing. Interesting, aren't they?'

'They sure are,' Peri peered curiously at the snaking plants. 'But what on earth can they be for?'

'At a guess, some sort of food supply,' he said. 'It looks to me as though they're pretty high in protein.'

Peri looked disgusted. 'You mean people eat those things?'

'Probably.'

'Yuk,' she said.

'Not really,' the Doctor said. 'You can cook almost anything, add a bit of this and a pinch of that, make it look attractive and it goes down a treat. Remaining alive is what matters. After all, the French eat snails, the Scots cope with tripe and sundry other people relish snakes and lizards, even grubs. It's all a matter of taste.'

Peri cast her eyes upwards and spread her hands in a gesture of defeat. 'I give up.'

But no matter how calm the Doctor remained, those plants looked fairly lethal to you. Nothing about them was appealing. As you looked close you could see that under each of the tendrils stretching so lovingly for the Doctor were two rows of suckers. They had to have a purpose, and it required no great stretch of the imagination to work out what it was. If they were to break through that glass, anything could happen, and probably would. It looked thick enough, but where was the guarantee? After all, you had no idea who had fashioned them. They could be people of an inferior culture. Space travel was no guarantee of advance, other than in one fairly narrow field.

'What,' you asked, 'do we do now?'

'Get out of here, I hope,' Peri said, still putting as much distance as possible between herself and the jarred plants.

'You're always in a hurry,' the Doctor complained. 'When will you understand that *all* flora and fauna are of value to me in my research?'

There were times when the Doctor's obsessive interest in his research, blind as it made him so frequently to sundry perils, rode on your nerves. This was one such time. You had no idea where you were in either Space or

1

Time and here was he, pottering about as though nothing was of any particular importance. Your patience was wearing thin.

'I'll tell you all you want to know about those things,' you said.

'Oh?' The Doctor cocked an inquiring eye at you.

'Simple.' You took a fire axe from its bracket on the wall. 'I'll break open one of the jars.'

The Doctor looked consideringly at the axe in your hands, then at the jars. 'I wonder if that's a good idea or not?'

'Not!' Peri blurted. 'For heaven's sake, you don't know what those things are or what they might do. Leave well alone is what I say.'

You hefted the axe thoughtfully. It was very tempting to use it and have done with the whole thing. Life was sufficiently confusing without prolonged mysteries, and this one had a simple solution.

At that moment a door opened behind you and you all swung round. There stood a man carrying a metal cylinder which you took to be food for the plants. He was dressed very much as a twentieth-century sailor, even to the collar, which had long outgrown its original purpose of protecting the jacket from the greasy pigtails once worn. He gaped at you in astonishment.

This is a straight choice. If you decide to befriend the sailor, go to **6**.
If you decide to smash the jar near you, go to **11**.
If you decide to wait and see, go to **4**.

2

Peri stood quite still, her eyes fixed on the vat of boiling water. Clearly, whatever evil influence was at work on the ship now intended to get her. She inched backwards, then turned – to see you standing there.

2

'What is it?' you asked, not having seen what was happening, in fact having only just arrived.

'Look,' she whispered, indicating the vat.

Now you saw what was happening. 'Come away quickly,' you said. 'Come over here.'

She did so, obviously terrified. Not that you could be said to be filled with joy, either. All of this was getting beyond you. There was menace and murder in the air and no visible explanation for it. What it all meant you had no idea, but it would have pleased you mightily to get out of it. The Doctor had the key to escape, of course, but he was not one for walking away from things, more was the pity.

Peri stood beside you, still staring at the vat which had ceased moving the moment she stepped away. 'I've had enough of this,' she said. 'It's just one thing after another.'

'So've I,' you agreed. 'I'd mind less if we could see what we're up against. But there's nothing there, is there?'

'Only something trying to kill us all.'

You nodded. 'And looking as though it might succeed.'

'I'm scared,' she said. 'I don't want to be here any more.'

You agreed, then added, 'But how do we get out?'

'The Doctor?' she suggested tentatively.

You shook your head, having already pondered that possibility. 'He won't do it. His curiosity always gets the better of him, and it's doing so now.'

'Couldn't we persuade him?'

'How?' you asked. 'You know what he is – everything for the sake of scientific investigation. Nothing would tear him away from this. He's fascinated.'

'I suppose you're right,' she said in a small voice.

Then a thought struck you. 'If we wanted to go from here to the Leechen-hold, d'you think we'd have to go through the control room?'

Peri was puzzled, but answered, 'I shouldn't think so. I mean, it wouldn't make sense, would it?' She thought for a

moment. 'No. Because when I came out here I noticed corridors leading off. They must lead round the control room.'

'Right,' you said. 'I'll stay here and you go back to the others. Have a quiet word with the Doctor and tell him I'm in serious trouble. Get him back here and I'll persuade him to get us back to the TARDIS and out of all this.'

'But what if he won't listen?' she asked.

'He will.'

'OK.'

She set off and, before long, reappeared with the Doctor in tow. 'What is it?' he asked. 'What is this trouble Peri says you're in?'

'It's very simple,' you said levelly. 'We want out.'

The Doctor was baffled. 'Out?'

'Up, out and away, Doctor. This time we're in too much danger and Peri and I have had it. We want to go.'

'Do you, now?' The Doctor could be very obstinate. 'May I remind you that this is a scientific expedition and they all carry their own risks? I feel for you both, but I'd like to point out that you're only passengers. My duty to the Time Lords remains the same: to learn, to discover, to absorb. There has to be a meaning to existence and I intend to contribute my morsel to discovering what it is – no matter what the danger.' He drew himself up to his full height. 'We stay.'

'I thought you'd say that,' you said, then produced the wooden stave you'd been holding behind your back and felled him, fill you with regret though it did.

Peri and you lifted his recumbent form and carted him out, no easy task. It had been a sorry thing to do. The Doctor had always been your close though eccentric friend. It gave you no pleasure to see his head lolling and his mouth hanging open. You prayed you hadn't done him a serious injury. Your aim had been good, and you weren't looking forward to his reaction when he finally came round.

3

After carrying him up several blind alleys, you located the TARDIS, took the key from the Doctor's pocket and got him inside. Once there, you both laid him gently down. Peri closed the door and you hit every button within sight.

Finally came the sighing and moaning sound and you knew you had dematerialized. You didn't know where you were going but, frankly, you didn't care.

Well, that's that. Burrigan and his crew have been left behind and you have ended an adventure.
To continue with it, go to **13**.

3

The Doctor was first off the mark. Taking advantage of his nearness to Tedder, he sprang forward with remarkable speed and knocked the lieutenant's gun down. 'Help the Commander,' he shouted.

You went to Burrigan's side. He had now drawn his own gun and looked as though he meant to use it. This would be sheer foolishness, you could see, as the Doctor and Peri also joined you; the crew also had armed themselves.

Tedder was now recovered from the Doctor's attack on him. 'Put the gun away,' he said.

'And surrender to you?' Burrigan replied. 'Not a chance.'

'Then what do you suggest?'

'I suggest you stop this foolishness and put your guns away.'

Tedder raised an eyebrow. 'And go through all that trouble again? You're a stubborn man, but this time you lose.'

'I suggest a strategic withdrawal,' the Doctor murmured to Burrigan. 'That way we might remain alive.'

The Commander nodded. 'For the moment the ship is in your hands,' he said to Tedder. 'We're going to leave you to it and see just what a mess you can make of it. And one word of warning: if anyone attempts to fire on us, the first dead man will be you.'

You saw Tedder pale. 'Hold your fire,' he said to his supporters. 'Let them go. They can't harm us now.'

'No,' Burrigan said. 'That'll come later.'

'*Much* later,' Tedder said. 'I take it you're leaving us now.'

Burrigan indicated the door leading to the hold and the four of you backed towards it, much aware of the guns trained on you. Burrigan waited until the three of you had left, then came out himself and pulled the door to behind him. 'We'll go into the hold,' he said, holstering his gun.

'And then?' you wanted to know.

'I get some time to think,' he said. 'I've never had a mutiny before and, by God, I'm not putting up with one now.'

'We might also see what materializes,' the Doctor said. 'All this can't have been for nothing.'

'No,' Burrigan agreed. Something's out to take over this ship and it might prove to be more than Mister Tedder bargained for.'

'I'd put my money on it,' the Doctor observed.

'Come on,' Burrigan said and led the way towards the hold. You all followed.

Tedder, meanwhile, was addressing the crew. 'Gentlemen,' he said. 'We're confronted here with something we don't understand. But it's been responsible now for three deaths. I want no more, and I'm sure you don't. I believe we can save ourselves and the ship by simply co- operating with whatever it is. Does anyone disagree?'

No one did, so he raised his head and spoke as to the air. 'We are willing to help you. Tell us what it is you want and we'll do it.'

And that strange cooing sound came again. It was gentle, yet somehow chilling.

But not as chilling as what came in through the door which

was opened. It was the first dead man, Todd. He looked hale and hearty enough, but when last seen he had been in an extreme state of death. To say that everyone was shaken would have been to put it mildly. They were riveted by the sight of what had been, to all intents and purposes, a dead man now walking. He smiled upon them all. 'Nice to see you again, mates.'

Tedder was first to find his voice. 'But you're dead.'

'I can understand your feelings on the matter,' Todd said. 'No pulse, no heartbeat, no flow of blood. To all intents and purposes, finished. But, as you can see, here I am.'

This was beyond Tedder's comprehension. 'But how? Why?'

'Yours not to ask questions,' Todd said. 'Yours but to do as you're told. And I'm the only one who's telling you what to do.' He turned to the crew. 'Get to your stations.'

'Just a minute,' Tedder objected. 'I'm not aware that a member of the crew is permitted to give orders to his mate.'

'Is that right?' Todd stepped towards Tedder and suddenly slapped him powerfully across the face, sending the lieutenant reeling across the cabin, to fetch up against the console. 'Now you know he is. You also know that if you don't do as you're told you'll get a good deal more trouble than that. Do you understand me?'

The shocked lieutenant rubbed the side of his face where the blow had landed, but could see that he was on a loser. How do you argue with a dead man as powerful as this one clearly was? But there might be a way. He lunged for his gun.

'Don't bother,' Todd said, almost wearily. 'You can shoot holes through me and it won't make a scrap of difference. Just do as I say and obey orders.'

Tedder straightened. 'Very well.'

Todd sighed. 'There's a sensible fellow.' Then he smiled, opened his mouth and cooed. It was weird to hear that dove-like sound coming from such a big man, especially one presumed dead.

3

'*Aran* calling,' came a voice from the speaker. 'Come in, please. *Aran* calling.'

Tedder made no move.

'Answer it,' Todd ordered.

'And let you take her over as well?' Tedder asked, obstinacy riding into his voice. 'It might be that we'll suffer, but we don't have to wish it upon others.'

'Which isn't necessarily the case,' Todd said. 'For all you know, the *Aran* might be the only way out of the fix you're in.'

'But I doubt it,' Tedder said. 'You're out to take her over as well.'

Todd sighed yet again. 'Then I'll tell you how to find out. Answer the *Aran*, tell her all is well and bring her in. And I'll tell you something else. If you don't, you'll regret it—as will your men.'

Tedder was beaten and he knew it. Watched by the crew, he crossed to the console. Todd smiled tolerantly. 'Who's a clever boy, then?' It was not a question. It was pure sarcasm.

You and your companions found yourselves among the jars of Leechen. As usual, they swayed hungrily towards you. But your situation was such that this was a matter of no importance. What was important was that none of you had the faintest idea of what was going on in your absence. That Tedder intended surrendering the ship you knew, but the question was: to what? Yours was an uneasy position, and you could see that it did not ride lightly on Burrigan's shoulders. His jaw was set and his expression murderous.

'We'll try the emergency steering,' he said.

'That's been tried,' Peri stated. 'And we all know what happened then.'

Burrigan was desperate. 'Then we'll try it again.'

'I wouldn't,' the Doctor said. 'I don't think they'd permit it.'

'But they can't be everywhere,' Burrigan objected.

'They do appear to be.'

'Am I supposed to stand here helpless while my ship is taken from beneath me?'

The Doctor's voice was quiet. 'For the time being, yes.'

Burrigan stood in bitter frustration. You could see that he could not take much more of this. All things considered, it was not within you to blame him. His shoes were for him; you would rather not be in them. The humiliation, you knew, would be more than you could bear. It was all very well for Peri, the Doctor and you to take things as they came and try to wrestle with them, but this man had been belittled.

'Hey, look over there!' Peri suddenly whispered.

You all turned to where she was pointing, and there stood a being no more than a little over a metre tall. It had a face like that of a doll, sweet, cherubic, enchanting. Curly blonde hair topped the tiny head. It wore a green outfit of immaculate cleanliness. In its left hand was clutched a device apparently made of shreds of wire.

'Isn't he beautiful?' Peri said.

'And where did he come from?' Burrigan wanted to know.

This was a question very much to the top of your mind as well. You'd been told of the vagaries of space travel, but this was getting ridiculous. You travelled with the Doctor and had a vague grasp of how it came about that you appeared here, there and everywhere. But the Doctor was a Time Lord and needed no explanation. Other beings appearing apparently from nowhere was something with which you were not prepared to contend. And a doll-like being such as this? What, precisely, was going on here? There was no answer, at least not immediately.

'You little darling,' Peri said. She bent over and moved towards it, a soothing hand before her. 'Come and talk to Peri.'

'Stay away!' the Doctor shouted. 'Stay away, Peri!'

But he was too late. The being moved like lightning, left hand striking out at the girl, and she reeled back, clutching her face where four claw-like marks had been torn down it.

'It's an Imp,' the Doctor said. 'A universal force of evil. Are you OK?'

3

Peri located her handkerchief and held it to her wounds, nodding wordlessly. Burrigan, meanwhile, was reaching for his gun, but the Doctor waved him away. 'Don't do it, Commander. That thing can move much faster than you.'

They waited to see what the Imp would do. It gave them a lovely smile, then turned its weapon in the direction of the jars.

'No,' Burrigan cried. 'You don't know what you're doing.'

But he was too late. There was a flash from the gun and a shattering of glass as the jar sundered. Immediately the Leechen tendrils began to fumble their way outwards.

Now decide what you want to do.
If you decide to wait and see, turn to **26**.
Should you decide to attack the Imp in order to protect your friends, turn to **10**.
If you attack the Leechen, turn to **17**.

4

You were equally surprised. He looked like something from a bygone age. So what was he doing on a spaceship? You had no time to dwell on it, because he dropped the cylinder and bolted through the door, fastening it behind him.

'Have I gone mad?' Peri asked. 'I could swear I just saw a sailor.'

'You saw a man dressed *like* one,' the Doctor said. 'There is a difference.'

'Either way,' you said, aware of the axe still in your grasp, 'do I break this jar or not?'

The Doctor considered for a moment. 'I think not. I'd love to examine them properly, but they must be trapped in those jars for a reason. It might be quite an innocent one, but why tempt fate?'

'Then how do we get out of here?'

'I don't think we have to worry about that,' the Doctor

answered. 'That sailor will have set all the alarm bells ringing. We won't be alone for long.'

And you weren't. The door opened and the first matelot came in with two others. All carried guns which were obviously advanced weapons. One was an officer, his rank proclaimed by shoulder-flashes.

'Don't move,' he said.

'My dear fellow,' the Doctor said. 'We have no intention of doing any such thing. And anyway, where could we go? We're marooned on your ship. I don't know where we are, but I'd be willing to bet that taking a nice walk outside is not an option.'

A quick glance told you that the TARDIS was out of sight in a corner of gloom. You were relieved. You knew how much confidence the Doctor had in the impregnability of his vessel, but unknown people poking about it was not something you particularly wanted. Too many questions might promote answers difficult to give.

'Who are you?' the officer asked in a distinct American accent.

The Doctor's voice was firm. 'Are you the commanding officer?'

'I am First-Lieutenant Tedder.'

Now you could place him. He was from Boston, speaking much as had the late President Kennedy. But he was blonde in colouring, so much so that at first glance he seemed to have no lashes or eyebrows. Strangely, his eyes were brown. The face in which they were set was thin and high-boned, the mouth firm.

'I'll speak to your Commander,' the Doctor said.

Tedder nodded and stood aside. He indicated the passageway beyond and you filed out, the guns following you as you did so. Pipes led in all directions, highly polished where they weren't painted. The hum of the air supply provided a constant background. All that was needed was the vibration of engines and a slight pitching and you could indeed have been at sea. But you knew you were not. The equipment you could see was too advanced for that.

You emerged into the control room. It was an extraordinary mixture of the traditional and the technological. Forward, a man stood at a timber steering-wheel, but there was no window before him. Instead there were banks of instruments, computers clicking quietly away and a row of video screens, in which you could see the stars hanging in space. It was evident that, though the ambience was that of the nineteenth and twentieth centuries, this ship was capable of things undreamed of then. To you, the steering-wheel itself looked more like dressing than a necessity, supported as it was by so much instrumentation.

To the side was a large metal desk. Its top was of glass, beneath which even more machinery glowed and flickered. Behind the desk sat a broad-shouldered man, his shoulders decorated with numerous flashes to indicate his rank. His dark hair and beard showed signs of greying. The set of his mouth brooked no argument, though his face was expressionless and his eyes cold.

Tedder stood rigidly to attention. 'These people were found in the hold, sir.'

'Very well, Mister.' His voice was deep, the sort that could effortlessly make itself heard over some distance. He had not taken his eyes off you and you had the uneasy feeling that he was looking right into your mind. 'Now, just who the hell are you?'

The Doctor introduced you, then waited. The Commander was clearly in no hurry. 'And might I ask what you are doing on my ship?' he said finally.

'It's quite inadvertent,' the Doctor said. 'We're time-travellers and I made an error of judgement somewhere.'

The Commander's voice remained calm. 'You are what?'

'Time-travellers.'

'You certainly did make an error of judgement if you expect me to believe that.'

The Doctor also was cool. 'Nonetheless, it remains a fact.'

'Does it? So one minute you can be in one century and the next, in another.'

'You put it simply but well.'

'Do I look like a fool?'

'Of course not.'

'Then try not to take me for one. It makes me testy.' He leaned his head on his hand. 'If you were to appear in the past and even so much as speak to someone, then you would alter the sequence of events from there on. Therefore, the present would turn out to be different from what it is. If you even stepped on an insect, everything would change. And when you returned to your future, it would be different from the one you left. Do you follow me?'

'Yes.'

'And?'

'Your logic is impeccable but inaccurate. You are operating within the parameters of your understanding. I am not. Forgive me for drawing attention to it, but I understand more than you because I am not of your time. I am from the misty realms of Time, and to explain the theory and practice of my form of travel would be more than I'd care to attempt.'

The Commander sighed. 'I see.' He stood up and you could see what an imposing figure he was, more than two metres in height and looking to be almost the same across the shoulders; not a man to argue with. 'Well, despite the nonsense you talk, you're here. There's nothing to be done about that. So we carry you. But mark me; I expect you to help with duties, if and when needed.' He came round the desk and surveyed the three of you, still betraying no emotion. 'I am Commander Burrigan. Should I tell you to do something, you do it and you do it fast. We are carrying

an emergency supply of food to Venus. Theirs was wiped out by an unknown virus, and if we don't help them soon the colony will no longer exist.'

'Is that what those awful plants are?' you asked. 'Those things in jars?'

'Yes,' Burrigan replied. 'The plants are called Leechen. They are high in protein and also high in risk. Let free in an oxygen atmosphere they will grow at a speed almost beyond belief, devouring everything they encounter until nothing is left. Then they devour themselves.'

'How do they control them on Venus?' Peri asked.

'Venus has no oxygen,' Burrigan answered. 'The plants are cultivated outside and fed just enough to keep them growing sufficiently to satisfy the demand. Now.' He turned away. 'You'll be taken to a cabin for the time being. Kindly stay from beneath our feet.'

The Doctor gave you a quick glance, which you interpreted correctly. 'I'll stay,' you said.

Burrigan turned on you and you felt the full force of his personality. It hit you like a physical blow. 'You'll stay? Why?'

'To help,' you said. 'I don't mind what I do. I just don't want to be locked up in a cabin.'

He regarded you for a moment. 'Can you clean brightwork?'

'With the best,' you said. 'Just give me some metal polish and a rag and see for yourself.'

'I shall.'

He nodded to a crew member, who took you to one side while Peri and the Doctor were taken away to their cabin. The crew member was Charlie. All that could be said for him was that he had lank hair, a prominent nose, protruding teeth and bad breath. Apart from that, he had nothing going for him. You turned your head away as he pressed exactly what you asked for into your hands. 'Polish everything you see that shines,' he breathed into your flinching face, 'then tell me what you're doing in this Jonas ship.'

You shook the can of metal polish and soused some onto the rag. In front of you was some copper piping. You set to on that, first rubbing the cleaner in. 'Jonas?' you whispered.

'Burrigan,' Charlie said. 'None of us trusts 'im. He's been in two disasters. First time, 'is ship was seriously damaged. Second 'e lost it altogether and 'ad to get 'ome in a space shuttle. There's a few dead men wouldn't speak too well of 'im, I tell you, mate. They're in deep space somewhere, or what's left of 'em. But does 'e care? I ask yer.'

'Right, mate,' said the man next to him. 'The sooner we land this load of rubbish on Venus and get 'ome again, the better off we'll be.'

'Rubbish, is it?' Charlie said. 'Then you'd better start praying that "rubbish" don't get free, because if it does, mate, we're all finished.'

'All I want is my danger money,' the man said. 'I pick it up and I'm finished with space-sailin' for ever.'

'Hah,' Charlie jeered through his sour teeth. 'I know your sort, mate. Two months of wine, women and song and you're back on the space jetties again lookin' for a berth. Just make sure you don't find Jonas Burrigan. Next time 'e'll prob'ly be carryin' a colony o' lepers.'

But Tedder loomed up behind you. 'Get on with your work,' he snapped. 'The next man I find talking gets twenty-four hours in the paint locker *without* bread and water.'

Charlie muttered something beneath his halitosis, but you noticed that he kept his head averted and buckled to at his cleaning. You did the same.

A crackling sound came from the speakers placed about the area. The one you took to be the radio operator tuned his dials, then looked up at Burrigan. 'Venus coming in, sir.'

'Very well.' Burrigan strode to the control console and flicked a switch, then waited.

4

'Venus calling *Medusa*, Venus calling *Medusa*,' came from the speakers.

'Hearing you loud and clear, Venus,' Burrigan answered. 'How are you coping?'

'We're still alive, Commander, but can't say much more than that. We have a number of sick now and they're increasing. It's difficult to keep going on the little rations we can allow. We've cut down physical movement as much as possible, but there's a limit to that. What's your position now?'

Burrigan glanced at the console. 'We're in area Victor One Three Two of region Dengra and closing fast.'

'Roger. But I doubt it's fast enough.'

'How long can you last?'

'No more than a week. After that we start to die.'

The Commander studied the console for a moment, then flicked more switches for further readings. 'I can boost our speed by burning off some of our safety reserve. That should get us to you in time.'

You could not help but notice the uneasy glances exchanged between the crew members. 'Safety reserve', you knew, meant exactly what it said. It was carried in excess of the fuel required for the voyage and was solely for use in an emergency. Burning it off unnecessarily left the ship and its crew in jeopardy. But then, the people of Venus were themselves experiencing an emergency and Burrigan was the man to decide what was to be done about that.

'Yes, I can do that,' he said. 'We'll be in contact later.'

'Thank you, Commander,' Venus replied. 'Our lives depend upon you and your men.'

'We'll be there. Out.' He turned from the console. 'Stand by for a five-second burn.'

Several of the crew jumped to their controls, but Burrigan was stopped short by a call from the radar tracker. 'Unidentified object heading directly towards us, sir.'

'Bearing?'

4

'Starboard thirty-two and closing fast.'

'What does it look like?'

'Could be a meteorite, sir. I can't get a visual on it yet.'

'Port twenty,' Burrigan snapped. 'Burn-off in five seconds. Start counting now.'

The helmsman spun the wheel and you saw the stars begin to slide across the screens.

'Five seconds to burn-off,' a crew member called. 'Four. Three. Two. One.' The ship shuddered as the propulsion unit flamed into life and thrust it forward. 'We have burn-off. Four. Three. Two. One.' Silence fell. 'Burn-off completed.'

'Very well.'

'Object still heading for us,' the tracker called. 'It is a meteorite, sir.'

'Meteorites can't change course at will,' Burrigan said. 'Look again.'

'I am looking, sir. I've got it on visual now.'

Burrigan crossed and looked at the tracker's screen. His face, as ever, remained impassive as he studied this remarkable sight. You, too, could see it now. As far as you could make out it bore all the appearance of what the tracker had said it was. But how could it change direction?

'Hard a-starboard,' Burrigan said.

'Hard a-starboard,' The helmsman spun the wheel.

You all stared at the tracking screen. Sure enough, the meteorite also changed course. 'We're on collision-course, sir,' the tracker said in a worried voice.

'I see that.' Burrigan swung away. 'All hands to emergency stations.'

The sound of the alarm siren whooped through the air. Men raced this way and that to their stations. Even Peri and the Doctor reappeared, wondering what was going on.

'Check safety shield!' Burrigan ordered.

'Safety shield secure, sir,' came the answer.

'Meet her,' he said to the helmsman.

4

'Aye, aye, sir.' The helmsman spun the wheel and steadied the ship on her original course. 'Ship steady.'

'How long have we got?' Burrigan asked the tracker.

'About thirty seconds, sir.'

'All secure yourselves,' Burrigan said. 'This might be quite a bump.'

Everyone grabbed hold of something, you included. Silence fell. You noticed that the Doctor, as full of curiosity as ever, had placed himself near the tracking screen and was watching it in fascination. Peri was hanging on to a stanchion.

'Ten seconds,' the tracker said, buckling his safety harness. 'Five.'

You waited. Burrigan glanced about to make sure that all were as secure as they could be, then gripped a bar on the front of the console. There was an almighty crash. The ship seemed literally to jump to one side.

The lighting dimmed. Everything shuddered before your eyes. The stars jumped across the video screens. Everyone clung on grimly. Then there was silence. The lighting returned.

'Damage reports,' Burrigan ordered, then to the helmsman, 'Can you get her back on course?'

'She's answering to the helm, sir.'

'Then do it.' He turned his attention to the videos scanning the ship's hull. You could see that the meteorite, although travelling at tremendous speed, had been quite a small one, about a quarter the height of the ship's side. Something like half of it adhered to the metal. It looked to be much like a boulder, a chunk of disintegrated planet, you thought, that had been bowling through space for aeons. You wondered if it were possible that the *Medusa* had about it some sort of gravity field that had drawn the meteorite in. It seemed unlikely, but what other explanation was there for a piece of rock that apparently steered itself through space? You glanced at the Doctor. If anyone would know, it was him.

4

But he was still absorbed in the video pictures, submerged somewhere in his own thoughts, as was so often the case.

Tedder reported to Burrigan. 'A slight leak amidships, sir. Quite small because of the shield. But it'll have to be seen to.'

'Very well, Mister. Get the repair crew into their space suits. And I want rid of that piece of rock stuck on the hull. We'll have trouble landing with that in the way.'

'Aye, aye, sir.' He hesitated. 'There is one problem, sir.'

'Which is?'

'Two repairmen are in sick-bay, one recovering from an appendix operation and one with a broken arm.'

'Then make up their number from the rest of the crew. We only want tool-carriers. Anyone can do that.'

'Right, sir.'

Now you have a choice. Should you volunteer to help or not?
If you do, then go to **18**.
Or you can take a chance. Roll two dice. If you score less than 8, go to **7**.
If you score 8 or above, go to **9**.

5

Something about the Doctor's attitude arrested your attention. He was too quiet, too introspective. He knew more than he was admitting to, or if he didn't know, then embryo suspicions were forming in his mind. He was the man to stay with, apart from which, though he was your mentor, you had a certain protective attitude towards him. Brilliant he was, and certainly beyond your comprehension, but there were times when his mind went off at tangents while reality pursued its remorseless straight line onwards. At such times he resembled little more than a bumbling idiot. That was when you had to stay; the dividing-line between genius and idiocy is a very fine one. You knew on which side he stood, but how many others did?

Peri nodded in the Doctor's direction. 'He's gone away again, hasn't he?'

'Yes,' you said. 'I wonder where?'

'No doubt we'll find out in the fulness of time.'

'Provided that isn't too far away. I don't like this at all.'

She gave you a cool look. 'You think I do?'

The Doctor's head was cocked to one side and he was nodding to himself. Something was coming through, but you knew better than to ask what it was. As Peri had said, time would reveal all.

'*Aran* calling, sir,' the radio operator said.

Burrigan switched on his extension. 'Come in, *Aran*. Commander Burrigan here.'

'Hello, Commander. Wingfield here.'

'Good to hear from you. How's your progress?'

'We're on full boost and tracking you. But there is one problem.'

Burrigan's expression was ironic. 'Only one?'

'It's quite serious, old man. I don't know if you're aware of it, but your course keeps varying. Holding to you is proving difficult.'

'We are aware of it. We're quite unable to keep anything steady. I suspect we've got some stowaways on board, though why they're causing all this trouble I can't imagine.'

'I wouldn't be too sure about stowaways,' the Doctor said, emerging from his thoughts. You all looked at him in some surprise.

'What else could it be?' Burrigan demanded.

'I think you've been invaded.'

'Invaded? In Heaven's name, by what? This ship is completely sealed, isn't it? There's no other way of travelling through space. So how could anyone possibly get in?'

'I'm not sure yet,' the Doctor answered. 'But that's my theory. And we don't have to think in terms of normal life-forms. I've encountered plenty of others which would not fit that concept.' He shook his head. 'No, I'm fairly sure you've been invaded. By what, remains to be seen.'

Burrigan surveyed him for a moment, then turned back to the console. 'Did you hear that, *Aran*?'

'We did. It sounds a bit far-fetched to me.'

'Me, too. But on the other hand, there has to be a cause.'

'Yes, but it could be mechanical. After all—'

The voice broke off, then there was a scream of the most dreadful agony, garbled and meaningless sounds, a pause, then that strange cooing sound you'd heard before. Then silence.

'Come in, *Aran*,' Burrigan said. 'Come in, please. Are you all right?' All that could be heard was static.

'She's switched off, sir,' the operator said.

'Very well. Keep trying to raise her.' He turned to the Doctor. 'I take it you have a theory for this as well?'

'Oh, yes,' the Doctor said. 'Now you've both been invaded.'

'And I repeat, by what?'

The Doctor shook his head. 'A theory is one thing, a guess is another. If you'll forgive me, I'd rather not guess.'

Tedder had re-entered, as had most of the crew. 'No trace of the body, sir, I'm afraid.'

'Very well, Mister.' He eyed the dials, gauges and computer readings on the console. 'Keep trying to get the pressure steady in the hold. If one of those jars breaks we'll have more trouble than we can cope with. And you,' he said to the helmsman, 'do the best you can to hold us on some sort of course.'

'I'm not having much luck, sir.'

'Then find some.' Now he turned to Peri. 'Would you like to do something useful, young lady?'

'Sure.'

'Go into the galley and make us all some coffee, would you? We could all use some.'

'OK. Where is the galley?' She didn't like being ordered about but it was an excuse to explore.

He pointed. 'Through that door, third entry on the port side.'

Peri hesitated. 'Which side is port?'

Finally he smiled. 'To your left, facing for'ard. You will be going for'ard. All right?'

Peri nodded and left. Immediately Burrigan rounded on a junior officer. 'Lieutenant Jackson, I'd like you to go aft and see if you can keep us on-course with the emergency steering.'

'Aye, aye, sir.' The officer made to leave.

By now you were beginning to feel somewhat spare. A lot was going on and your contribution came to nil, so you volunteered to go with him. Burrigan nodded his assent and you set off with Jackson. Along the corridors you went and through the Leechen-hold to the emergency-steering cabin. You could not help but notice that the plants swayed towards you as you passed them.

Jackson put his hand on the lever of the door and paused. 'In view of all that's happened, we'll go carefully, shall we?'

You agreed wholeheartedly. Jackson raised the lever and gently eased the door open. You both looked in. All seemed well. Nothing stirred. Nothing appeared to be out of place.

'Looks good enough,' Jackson said. 'But we'll take care, just the same.' Cautiously he entered. You followed.

Peri, meanwhile, had located the galley. It was gleamingly clean, sparkling with chrome and stainless steel working-surfaces. The crockery, all made of some kind of clear material, was carefully racked up against the possibility of a jolt to the ship. Everything was secure and shipshape. There was nothing in sight to be criticized. Obviously, Commander Burrigan ran a tight ship.

The vat of boiling water was secured to the bulkhead above a sink. Sundry buttons indicated the varieties of tea, coffee and chocolate available. Another one, beside them, was for releasing cups singly. Trays were racked to the side. Peri extracted one and began buttoning out the cups while mulling over your circumstances. They were strange indeed, and she wondered how the Doctor had come to make the TARDIS materialize in a spaceship, of all things. Sometimes she doubted his ability. It was not that there was any question of his brilliance, far from it. But he could be erratic in his judgement. Really some of the situations in which he landed you all left a lot to be desired; peace of mind was in short supply, for a start. And look where you were now: in Outer Space with everything about you going mad. Sometimes the Doctor was tough to take.

Then there was the question of you. Oh, she had to admit that she liked you well enough, but you too had a tendency to dismount on both sides of the fence and ride off in all directions. Impetuous was the best word she could find to describe you. There was this tendency for you not only to go along with the Doctor, but even to jump onto some of his more extreme ideas and aid and abet them. A likeable character you had, in her opinion, but also certain flaws which one day could prove fatal. Why, for instance, did you keep drifting off into reveries at critical moments? In that respect you were as bad as the Doctor. And why did you hurl yourself into things so? Whence this enthusiasm? Heavens, she loved life, there was no denying that. But since such was the case, she went to considerable lengths to hang on to it, whereas you . . . Ah well, at least you were as good a companion as she could hope for, given the circumstances, and dear me, she had her own faults, not least a love for the Doctor. There she was, she decided, and all she could do was face up to everything, as did you and the Doctor.

So she did, and continued buttoning out the cups. But a sound from above her head froze her. She looked up. The bands securing the vat of boiling water to the bulkhead were slowly springing free. The vat was directly above her. If it fell and tipped its contents over her, all fifty litres of it, her future was assured. There wouldn't be one. She stared in horror as another bolt sprang free.

6

Now you go to a game of chance.
Take two dice and roll them until you come up with one of these scores. If the first score you get is 4 or below, go to **24**.
Should it be 5-9, go to **2**.
Should it be 10 or more, go to **13**.

6

You stared back for a moment, then lowered the axe and put it to one side. You held a hand before you. 'We are friends. We mean you no harm.'

He put down the cylinder and turned his bright blue eyes back to you. 'Who are you?'

You introduced yourselves and he hesitated in caution, then came forward. 'And how did you get here?'

'That's not important,' the Doctor said. 'The question is, where are we?'

'You're on the spaceship *Medusa*.'

The Doctor nodded. 'I thought so. And where are we heading?'

'Nowhere.'

'Nowhere?' The Doctor stared at him blankly.

'Exactly,' the sailor said. 'This is more of a city than a ship. We've got all we need to exist in space indefinitely. Most of the food is grown hydroponically and then there are these.'

You noticed that he flinched when he indicated the plants. There was something wrong here. He was a burly man with an open face and red hair, not the sort to be easily cowed. Yet he kept his gaze away from the jars. Why should that be? Certainly their appearance had nothing to commend it, but they were contained and apparently safe. 'What are these plants?' you asked.

'Leechen,' he said, still not looking at them.

'And their purpose?' the Doctor asked.

'Food for the Xan.'

'I knew you had to be right,' Peri said to the Doctor.

6

She turned back to the sailor. 'But what sort of people are the Xan if they eat muck like that?'

'They aren't people,' the sailor said. He drew nearer and lowered his voice. 'They look like us physically, but they aren't like us in any other way. I'll tell you what happened.'

He rubbed a hand across his forehead and drew in his breath. 'I used to live in a tiny village called Brightford. In Hampshire, that was. I ran a garage. There wasn't a lot of business, but it was enough to keep us ticking over. And it was a good life. Everybody knew everybody else, and if you had any problems there was always somebody ready to help. In fact, when I look back now I can see that we didn't know how happy we were. We thought it was dull and routine, but there's a lot to be said for that. We can see it now that it's too late. See, one night the whole area was lit up by a brilliant light in the sky above us. We couldn't make out what it was at first – we thought it might be a helicopter shining a searchlight on us – but then it faded a bit and we saw this disc-shaped thing coming down onto the common. Big it was, and we figured what we were seeing was a flying saucer. Well, for all I know that's what it was. But it didn't mean us any good, I can tell you. The next thing we knew was that armed men poured out of it and surrounded those of us who were watching. Then others went into every house and forced the people out. It was terrible to see. Some of them were elderly and weak, but they had to come, just the same. One of the things the Xan don't know anything about is mercy. And they looked frightening enough, God knows, in their black uniforms and metal headpieces. Mrs Forbes died of a heart attack the moment they burst in on her, poor old thing. But at least she didn't have to face up to what we do now, there's that to be said for her.'

'And what is it that you have to face up to?' you asked. But the sailor ignored you.

'We were herded aboard, then brought up to this vessel,' he went on. 'Then we sailed back into space again and

6

learned our fate. They put us all into these uniforms and made us do the menial tasks – like I look after feeding the Leechen.' He shuddered again. 'They treat us well and keep us fed. But there's always a catch, isn't there?'

'What?' the Doctor asked coldly.

The sailor licked his lips nervously. 'We're food for the Leechen. There aren't many of us left now.' He looked sardonically at your group. 'They'll be glad to see you, believe me.'

You were chilled and Peri gasped. Yet the sailor went on. 'And don't think of escape. We're watched all the time and when we aren't working, we're locked in cells. Believe me, it's hopeless.'

You could see that it was. Using all the eloquence you could muster, you persuaded the Doctor to return you all to the TARDIS, the sailor with you. Off you went again into time and space and this was one adventure you didn't have.

The sailor simply wanted to desert and you have inadvertently helped him.
Don't believe everything you hear.
Try again, go to **4**.

7

Two of the crew were detailed off by Tedder and the repair crew stepped into the air-lock, tools and crowbars in their hands. Burrigan remained with his eyes fixed to the video screens. Strangely, the Doctor was only watching Burrigan. Why was he doing that, you wondered? Surely, what was going on outside was of more vital interest. You could see the repair men moving in towards the meteorite and the welder locating the fractured seam. If the ship was ever going to reach Venus in time, all depended upon their efforts. So why watch Burrigan?

You edged close to Peri. 'What's the Doctor up to now?' you asked.

Peri followed your gaze and shrugged. 'When you can explain how his mind works, let me know. I gave up long ago.'

That advanced the cause not at all. It could be said to have retarded it. The Doctor was difficult enough to understand at the best of times, but to have Peri shrugging him away like that only increased the mystification. But still he watched Burrigan and ignored the videos.

Burrigan turned to Tedder. 'Have you checked the hold, Mister?'

'Yes sir. No damage. The Leechen are still contained.'

'Yes, and one more collision like that and they won't be, will they?'

'The jars are sturdy, sir.'

'So am I. But that doesn't make me infallible, does it?'

Tedder bowed his head. There was no answer to a question like that.

'Well, Mister?' Burrigan persisted.

'The jars are secure, sir,' Tedder said. 'They are in no danger.'

And suddenly Burrigan blew his top. So that was what the Doctor had been waiting for. '*They* may be in no danger, but *we* are!' he shouted.

'Keep calm,' the Doctor interjected. 'Remember your mission. The people on Venus are utterly dependent upon you.'

'And they aren't going to see me,' Burrigan roared. 'I've risked my men and the ship quite enough for one voyage. Why didn't they send two ships out, or even three? Then we could have supported each other. But no, they insisted that I could do it alone. Really? I've had two vessels sink into deep space beneath me and it isn't going to happen again.' He rounded on the Doctor. 'D'you know what they call me, you mysterious idiot who claims to travel in Time?' His face purpled. 'Jonas! Jonas! Me – the best Commander in the whole merchant space fleet, a damned Jonas. I've had enough. This whole accursed expedition ceases now. We're going back to Earth.' He turned back to Tedder. His eyes were bulging and you, for one, knew there was no arguing with him. His senses had left him. The strain had all been too much. But he was still the Commander. 'Get the men back in, and do it now.'

'Aye, sir,' Tedder moved to the microphone and began to murmur orders to the men outside. You noticed that they showed no reluctance to return. Nor, indeed, did any of the men still inboard show any hesitation in obeying the Commander's orders. You supposed they had been paid a danger bonus for such a mission, but they were quite willing to forfeit it if their Commander so chose.

'Full about,' Burrigan told the helmsman. 'Steer for Earth. Mister Tedder will give you an exact course shortly.'

'Full about, sir.' The helmsman spun the tiller. He showed no hesitation either. Probably he had a wife and children at home. Whatever the way of it, he would rather be with them than where he was.

'Sir, you can't land the *Medusa* with half a meteorite attached to the side,' Tedder protested. 'The balance will be wrong for the descent.'

'I don't propose to descend, Mister,' Burrigan snapped. 'There's any number of space shuttles loitering about outside the Earth's orbit. We'll dock in one of them.'

The repair crew emerged from the air lock. They began to remove their space-suits, to place their tools to one side. Tedder watched them in some dismay. He turned to his Commander. 'Sir, the Venus colony will want to know why we've turned back.'

Burrigan stared bleakly at him for a moment, then took a crowbar from one of the repairmen. He crossed to the radio, hefted the bar and brought it smashing down on the set. 'Now they won't be able to find out, will they? he said.

Tedder was lost for words. He had lost. Commander Burrigan had gone mad. And yet, though it was in his mind to mutiny, he knew that the crew was a reluctant one and it was just possible that Burrigan was right. He had commanded spaceships for years. He had been in disasters. His judgement was to be respected. Furthermore, every vessel had only one man in command. He had no desire to be involved in the equivalent of a Caine Mutiny. He did as he was told.

You and your friends could do nothing but stand by and observe. 'Whatever you do, keep quiet,' the Doctor whispered to you and Peri. 'The strain's been too much for the man.'

'He's gone right off his trolley,' Peri replied. 'A man as unstable as that shouldn't be in charge of a spaceship.'

The Doctor shook his head. 'Too much time in Space takes its toll on anyone. He's had too much. That's all there is to it.'

And it was. Under Burrigan's command the *Medusa* made the return voyage to a space shuttle, from which you were all ferried back to Earth. There Burrigan was immediately sent to a psychiatric ward and the crew disbanded. What happened to the Venus colony you never heard, because there was nothing for it but to return to the TARDIS and move on.

You lost that time. For you the adventure is over.
To find out what actually happened go on to **9**.

8

You came to in the control room. The crew were about their duties, Tedder in charge. Leechen crawled its way here and there, but was being held at bay with machetes. You were lying on a bench to the side. When you stirred and sat up Tedder came across to you. 'Are you OK?'

You gently touched the back of your head. 'A little sore. What hit me?'

'One of the dead men, I should think.'

'But why?'

8

'Your guess is as good as mine. I don't understand any of this. But the *Aran*'s alongside and the walkway is connected. We expect someone to arrive at any moment.'

You stood up and joined the others in looking expectantly at the external door. Finally it opened and a young man came in. He was handsome but, oddly, wore make-up. He looked about him in mild surprise. 'Oh, dear,' he said. 'I've done something wrong, haven't I?'

'Like what?' Tedder asked.

'Well, I was rehearsing a play,' he said. 'All about the twenty-second century. Now it looks as though I'm in it.'

'You are,' you said. 'But which century are you from?'

'The twentieth.' He looked about him and brooded a moment. 'It's always been my trouble, you know. I identify too closely with the part I'm playing. I've been told off about if before. If I'm playing a policeman, then that's what I become; a vicar and I'm it. It's silly, really, but how else do you make your acting convincing?' He sighed. 'I've overdone it this time, haven't I? So far into the part that it's turned into reality.'

'You mean you aren't from the *Aran*?' Tedder demanded.

'If I knew what the *Aran* was I'd be able to answer you. Since I don't, I can't.'

Tedder shrugged his bafflement and turned away, to see the Imps still grinning at him. 'So much for our hopes of rescue. Help we need and what do we get?' His tone was scornful. 'An idiot actor from the twentieth century.'

'Oh, I say,' the young man protested.

But you were beside him. 'Don't take offence,' you said. 'Things are a little difficult here at the moment.'

'I see.' He put a gentle hand on your shoulder. 'For those words of comfort, my thanks.'

He should not have done that, because his touch transferred you to his place.

You were on a stage, surrounded by scenery depicting a spaceship. The other actors loitered about, scripts in their hands and looking as bored as actors usually do while waiting for their parts to come up. Backstage you could see a group of stage-hands playing cards. The whole atmosphere was one of concentration alleviated only by tedium.

The producer was addressing you from the auditorium. 'That isn't quite right, dear heart. Look, you and Luke are at bitter odds. That's what the script calls for, isn't it? Here you are, lost in Outer Space and with only enough food for one. It's you or him. That's all there is to it. Now remember, you both know it. The only difference is that Luke is a dreadful villain and you aren't. That's why he's going to try and get you with his knife. You foil him, but that comes later. For the moment, a little more bite in your voice. All right, darling?'

'Right,' you said and glanced again at your script to remind yourself of the lines. 'Shall we go now?'

'Please, sweetie.'

You squared up and confronted your fictional adversary, Luke. 'If we shorten our rations we can last a while longer,' you said, as per the script.

'And one of us alone could last even longer,' Luke replied.

'But we're both alive, aren't we?'

'For the moment.'

And suddenly he produced the fake dagger and lunged at you. But there turned out to be a problem. Without anyone's knowledge, the knife was faulty. The mechanism that allowed the blade to retract into the handle was jammed. So when the blade struck your chest it went in.

Blackness descended.

You've reached the end of the road.
It's a pity you didn't choose to go on to **23**.

9

Two men were detailed off and, space-suited and armed with their tools, the repair crew entered the air-lock, waited for the air to be withdrawn, then made their way outside. Their reports began to come in: the damage was minimal and the meteorite could fairly easily be prised away. Burrigan was relieved. Things could have been much worse. He ordered that the Leechen should be checked for safety and Tedder set off with two men to see to it.

You joined Peri and the Doctor. They were looking out of a view-port, the Doctor very thoughtful. All you could see was a piece of the meteorite still adhering to the side.

'Interesting?' you asked lightly.

'Very,' Peri said.

You looked again, noticing nothing in particular. 'What's so fascinating about a piece of rock?'

'The fact that it's hollow,' the Doctor said. 'I know your experience is limited, but mine isn't, and a hollow meteorite is something I've never encountered.'

You could see it now, the section that was visible smooth inside, almost as though it had been worked with tools. 'Is there something in there?' you wondered.

'Even if there were, how would it survive a crash like that?' Peri asked. 'Anyway, it's smashed to bits.'

But the Doctor was still pensive. 'The question is, does a Space vessel have to be constructed out of some sort of metal?'

'But, whatever it's made of, it would still need a propulsion unit, wouldn't it?' you said. 'And I don't see one.'

'You're assuming it was launched from a gravity field,' the Doctor said. 'That isn't necessarily the case.'

'But it followed us,' Peri pointed out. 'It was able to change course.'

'Indeed yes,' the Doctor nodded. 'That I find most intriguing.'

'Perhaps it was pulled in by our own gravity field,' you suggested.

'Possibly,' the Doctor said. 'But not necessarily probably.'

Burrigan was still issuing orders and ensuring that the ship was back on course, its speed remaining set to the boost he had given it. The crew were busy about their duties, calm now that the worst was over. Not that there had been any undue alarm; these were hardened Space-travellers who had learned to take things as they came. But a guided meteorite was something beyond their experience and not easily accepted.

Burrigan approached your party. 'Are you all right, Doctor?'

'Thank you, yes,' the Doctor replied, then, 'Do you mind if I ask what might seem to be an irrelevant question?'

'Fire away.'

'Well, it's this,' the Doctor said. 'This ship is obviously quite technologically advanced. Yet you have it rigged and manned as though you were at sea, even to the uniforms you wear. My guess is that everything would work most efficiently without anyone so much as lifting a finger. So why all this?'

A glint of amusement showed in the Commander's eyes. 'Psychology. The head-shrinkers found that men too long in deep space not only began to lose their identities but, to a certain extent, their minds as well. Nothing to do, you see, except for dictated exercises which soon came to appear pointless and boring. There are quite a few cases of people going totally insane. After all,' he indicated the view-port, 'you've only to look out there for a while to feel the vast emptiness creeping coldly into your soul, haven't you? So the clever men came up with the idea of a traditional uniform and the various ranks that go with it. Then they went even further and allocated tasks which, though not vital, give the men the feeling that they are performing important duties; in effect, that without them the ship wouldn't function.'

'And would it?' you asked.

'Not as we have it rigged at the moment. Not without the men performing their duties. But in an emergency we can switch everything into computer override. All we need then is one man hitting a keyboard. We try to avoid that, for obvious reasons.'

'Sound reasoning,' the Doctor said. 'And is that also the reason for the decor – nice, warm pastel shades?'

'You have it,' Burrigan nodded. 'Imagine how it would be if everything were bare metal or some ghastly institutional green. Wouldn't do much for morale, would it?' He swung away as the radio crackled again into life. 'Excuse me.'

'Venus calling *Medusa*,' came from the speakers.

'Hearing you loud and clear,' Burrigan said. 'Come in, please.'

'Are you still on course, Commander?'

'We are now. We had a small incident with a wandering meteorite. We've also increased speed.'

'Good. We've now fuelled up the spaceship, *Aran*, and she's blasted off. She'll let you know the point of interception.'

'Has she sufficient fuel?'

'More than you because the distance is shorter. If you can transfer some of the Leechen she can do a longer burn-off and be back here well ahead of you.'

'Good. We'll wait to hear from you.'

'There's just one thing, Commander: is the Leechen packed in jars tough enough to withstand transfer? We don't want any accidents.'

'I was told it was,' Burrigan replied. 'The jars have taken a shock or two so far. We can only hope for the best. Anyway, we have padded cranes.'

'Thank you, Commander. Please hold to your present course. We'll be in touch. Out.'

Burrigan stood for a moment in thought, his huge presence looming over the console, his mighty hands looking as though they could pick up every one of the instruments and crush them like paper decorations, which they probably could. It occurred to you that it was only such men as Burrigan who could lead their men into the vasty depths of infinite Space and bring them out not only alive but still possessed of their spirits. This was a man of more than physical power. This man was born to lead. He radiated such confidence and authority that it would have taken someone of considerable nerve even to question it.

His face betrayed not a flicker of indecision when the lights went down again. He remained rock-like at the console as the instruments went berserk, indicator-needles leaping this way and that and the chronometers spinning backwards as though time had lost all meaning. You were startled and not a little afraid, but he remained motionless, only saying to the helmsman, 'Hold your course.'

'Can't, sir,' the helmsman said. 'The instruments have gone potty.'

'Then do the best you can.'

'There's nothing I *can* do, sir.' There was fear in the helmsman's voice. 'The figures are a blur.'

And you could see that they were. What should have been stationary illuminated red figures in front of him were now a flickering confusion, now reading this, now reading that, but in no way reading anything that he could steer by. The man was in an impossible situation.

Burrigan stabbed a button. 'Gone into computer override.'

There was a pause while the helmsman studied the situation. 'It's still the same, sir,' he said. 'I can't make head nor tail of it.'

'Then don't try,' Burrigan said, hitting the button again. 'Override now off. Just do the best you can.'

He turned and surveyed the control room, his massive presence filling you with the conviction that if his control were to snap he would break everything in sight, which he probably could. Peri, the Doctor and you remained silent. The awesome power exuded by the Commander was sufficient to button any lip. This was no time for asking questions lightly. In fact, this was no time for doing anything other than stand in silence while the man waited for something to evolve. Like a rock he stood, as best you could see, his face set like stone and, as you certainly could feel, his mind as cold as a block of ice. This was no man to trifle with. This was one who could be confronted with anything and still have enough control and to spare to wait things out until he could make sense of, then deal with them. You had to hand it to the people on Earth; they certainly knew what it took to make a Space Commander and, beyond question, they knew where to find it. It was a matter of 'the right man, the right place, the right time'. Given any number of alternatives, you would have chosen to follow Burrigan. There was about the man an air of unuttered rage. And he kept his mind as much under control as he did his fury.

No man of such a temperament knows why he is so born. There is a fire in the belly, directed one knows not where. Possibly it is against life itself, the fact of having been born. The mark of the man is that he keeps it locked within. When it erupts it is in private. The fury is there, but so also is the intellect to contain it. Personal death is of no importance, but the survival of others is.

Such a man was Burrigan. You could not help but feel wonder as you watched him stand there as though he were carved out of rock. He was waiting. He was prepared to stand there for ever until something he could understand revealed itself. All the responsibility was his, and his soul was big enough to carry it. Alone he stood, and that was the way he liked it. External advice was neither needed nor welcome.

'What you are watching,' the Doctor said, 'is a perfect demonstration of how Man got as far as he did. Would you argue with him?'

You shook your head. 'No.'

'But why is he standing so still?' Peri asked.

'Because if he betrays so much as a morsel of fear,' the Doctor said, 'the crew will catch it. So he doesn't.' He thought a moment, then fixed you with a cold eye. 'You see, that man won't admit to fear. He's a born survivor. He'll only recognize physical pain as a warning from his body that something's wrong. That man is a born leader. He does what he's appointed to do and admits to no misgivings. I would not like to be his enemy.'

That made a great deal of sense. The sheer power of Burrigan filled the control room. There he stood, as if carved from rock, waiting for he knew not what, but totally immovable. No, you would not wish to be his enemy. He would tread you underfoot like an insect. Commander Burrigan was important. Commander Burrigan was a leader. Commander Burrigan took no rubbish from anyone, including himself.

The door opened and the party sent to inspect the Leechen came back in. But not in an orderly manner, because suddenly there was a flash of almost blue light. One of the men literally leapt from the floor, hands to his throat as he tried to tear the pain from his body. It was a useless effort. His hair raged like wire on his head. His eyes bulged. He screamed. He slumped like an empty sack. He was dead.

It didn't need the ship's doctor to prove it, either. He went through the ritual examination, but you could see that the man was gone. No one could be that ashen gray and survive. But what in heaven's name had killed him? It isn't every day that there's a bright flash and a man leaps into the air in the most awesome agony then falls dead. There has to be some explanation for it.

Burrigan asked, but there was none forthcoming. The medical man shook his head in mystification. The body had not been in contact with anything electrical. That being the case, there was no explanation for the brilliant flash. A tension of fear began to steal into you. Peri looked questioningly as the Doctor. The Doctor was outwardly calm, but you could see that his mind was beavering away at yet another problem.

'Get him out of the way,' Burrigan curtly said. 'He'll have a Space burial. But first I want to know what the hell is going on here.' He turned to Tedder. 'I want your report, Mister.'

'All's well, sir,' Tedder said. 'The jars are secure.'

Burrigan indicated the body now being hauled to the side. 'And that man?'

'I'm sorry, sir. I'm as puzzled as you are. For all I know, it could have happened to me.'

'And I'm beginning to think it's a pity it didn't. The best leaders lead from the front, Mister. Your men are always protected. The reason you're an officer is because you never require your men to do anything you won't do yourself.' Burrigan's face was now set like iron and his voice had the same ring about it. 'Why was he ahead of you?'

'I'm, sorry, sir.' Tedder was faced with unreason and knew it, though not how to cope. 'We just happened to come in that way.'

There was no avoiding the Commander's rage. 'In future, Mister, *you* go first. When in doubt, lead. And right now we are in doubt. Something's gone cockeyed and we haven't the remotest idea what it is. Until we find out you will behave properly. Do I make myself clear?'

'Yes, sir.'

You wished the anger could have been vented in private, but equally you knew that spaceships were designed in the same way as the old warships; the equipment came first, living accommodation second. Privacy was of secondary importance, if it even rated at all.

But, despite Burrigan's fury, you were still watching the Doctor, who appeared to be watching nothing at all, vanished into some internal reverie. You saw him glance briefly at the dead man, then tilt his head in a listening attitude. What was he hearing? Then you heard it too. It was a gentle cooing sound, as of a contented dove. But where was it coming from?

Now everyone could hear it. You could see the puzzlement on their faces. Birds in outer space? This was a total impossibility. You might as well go fishing in a furnace. But the sound was there and there was no denying it. Doves?

9

Burrigan looked at the faces about him. 'All right,' he said. 'So what is it?'

No one answered. Indeed, how could they? You looked a query at Peri and all she could do was shrug her bafflement back at you. This furthered the cause not at all. As for the Doctor, well, he might as well not have been there, enwrapped as he was in the mists of his vast and ever-curious mind.

Burrigan, however, still had all his wits about him. He still had control of the ship, and one of his gauges was sending him a message of warning. He looked again at Tedder, of whom he was no longer overly fond. It could have been said that his eyes looked like two metal studs. 'Are you looking after the pressure in the hold, Mister?'

'Yes, sir,' came the reply.

'Then why has it fallen ten points?'

Tedder looked amazed. 'Excuse me?'

'Ten points, Mister. Those things will implode if you leave them like that. *I am not losing this ship because you can't do your job*!' Now Burrigan's patience was beginning to leave him. He had hit a high. He'd had enough. The sight of Tedder was almost more than he could stand. You could see it in the murderous expression of his face. 'You will rectify this matter, Mister,' he said. 'Because if you don't, I'll have your hide for shoe-leather. Do you read me?'

Tedder read him, but not for too long. Not too often was Burrigan encountered in this mood. When he was, it was as well to avoid him. Burrigan was one who remained calm, self-controlled, to all appearances almost a loveable person. But always within him there remained that raging violence. It was best left alone. Tedder left it alone. You watched as he crossed to the pressure controls and adjusted them.

The pressure remained the same. 'It isn't answering, sir,' he said.

'I see that,' Burrigan replied. 'A malfunction, d'you think?'

'I've put the fail-safe on, but there's still no response.'

'I see.'

You all could see, but what was missing was an explanation. 'Nothing's infallible,' the Doctor commented.

'This is,' Brannigan said. 'There are so many fail-safe stages that the chances of an actual breakdown are millions to one against.'

The Doctor remained cool. 'That still leaves the one.'

And for no good reason a chronometer detached itself from the bulkhead and hurled itself across the area, narrowly missing Peri. She jumped aside. 'What on earth is happening now?'

What a very good question that was, because, all of a sudden, the air was full of flying objects. Fire-extinguishers, implements, internal speakers flew this way and that. Even the Commander's desk ran itself from one side to the other. His chair tipped itself over. Everyone cowered and dived for cover amid what had become a maelstrom. Death was in the air. The helmsman went down, smitten on the head by a flying radio. You noticed, even amid the pandemonium, that the moment his hands fell away from the helm, the computers switched into override, so Burrigan had been right in saying that nearly all the crew duties were non-essential.

For his own part, Burrigan stood like a rock. Nothing moved him, not even a flying pen-holder which struck him in the face. His ship had gone mad about him, and you could see that, though he could find no reason for it, he had no intention of giving in either.

'Could it be poltergeists?' Peri wondered, arms before her forehead.

You had no idea, but you could see the gauges spinning again and the clocks solemnly reversing time. Was something forcing you into another time-spin? Then the chaos stopped and everyone straightened, though admittedly with more than a little caution.

9

There was silence until Burrigan spoke. 'Right,' he said. 'Get this mess cleared up.'

Wordlessly, the crew did as ordered, but you could see their unease as they glanced continually about them for fear of another attack. Not that it was within you to blame them; if solid objects could hurl themselves about like that something was seriously amiss.

'How's the pressure in the hold, Mister?' Burrigan asked.

'Almost back to normal,' Tedder replied. 'But the indicator isn't holding steady.'

'Very well. Do the best you can.' Clearly Burrigan had recognized that there was no point in blaming others when confronted with the inexplicable. He only watched as the crew cleared up the shambles, making no attempt to tend to the gash on his face.

Peri tilted her head to one side. 'Do you have the feeling we're being watched?' she said.

The Doctor nodded. 'You feel it, too.'

'Very much so. But I don't see anything.'

You straightened, holding the chronometer you had picked up from the deck. You, too, paused, then you also felt the strange sensation of being observed. But by what? As Peri had said, the feeling was there. What, though, was causing it? You experienced a prickling up your back, then tried to shrug it off and carried the chronometer over to a side-bench.

At that moment the door leading to the hold burst open and a crew member rushed in, his face ashen. 'I've seen it, I've seen it!' he shouted.

But what he had seen you were not to find out, because at that moment there came the same bright flash and he was hurled into the air in writhing agony, to crash, dead, to the deck. You could feel the terror in the air as everyone stared, transfixed, at the fallen man.

But Burrigan was still very much in charge. He crossed and knelt beside the man to make sure that he was dead. There was no pulse. The eyes stared. Burrigan straightened.

'Put him to one side,' he said gently, then addressed the remainder of the crew, his voice cool. 'I want no panic, men. I know we can't yet explain what's happening, but until we do, no purpose will be served by permitting these troubles to divert us from our duty, which is to get to Venus. I intend to do precisely that, as I'm sure you do. I rely upon you as a fine crew.' He turned to Tedder. 'Would you please attend to this man, Mister?'

'Yes, sir.' Tedder gestured to two of the men and they gently lifted their friend and carried him away.

You all looked on in disbelief as they did so, utterly mystified by the occurrences.

'Call the *Aran*,' Burrigan said to the radio operator. 'Tell her we are having as yet unidentified trouble which might make us slower because holding to course is proving difficult. Ask her to make all possible speed.'

The operator juggled with his controls in obedience.

Tedder emerged from the side-cabin where they had taken the second dead crewman. There was a puzzled expression on his face. 'Sir, I have to report that the body of the first crewman, Ordinary Spaceman Todd, is not where we put it.'

Burrigan's eyes were cold. Puzzle was mounting upon puzzle. 'Then where is it?'

'We don't know, sir.'

'Then find it. It can't have gone far, can it?'

'No, sir.' He addressed the rest of the crew. 'Search the ship from top to bottom.'

The crewmen made off in various directions, but you could see that they would rather have remained together in the face of all they had experienced. But Tedder's orders came from Burrigan and the Commander was not a man they chose to disobey.

You have some options now.

You can help by accompanying Lieutenant Tedder. If you do that, go to **21**.

Or you can accompany a party of the crew members, in which case go to **20**.

Or you can remain with the Doctor and Peri to see what materializes. Do that, and go to 5.

10

You jumped at the Imp but he was too quick for you. His gun flashed and you were briefly in agony, then unconscious. . . .

To all intents and purposes it was a routine flight, crossing your own lines, then the enemy's, and looking out for undue troop-concentrations which could mean trouble. This, after all, was The War To End All Wars, and it was your intention to do all you could to see that your side won. It had started in a blaze of patriotism in 1914 and had not taken too long to descend into a carnage of horror, as first one side, then the other gained a few yards of territory at a terrible cost in human lives.

Gone was the idealism and the heroism of fighting for one's country. All that remained was the bitter and ugly existence of the troops in the trenches beneath you, struggling as they were against mud, rats, machine guns, rifles, constant shelling and a realization that the Germans were as determined to win as was your own side. Not that the generalship was all that good, either. It took a special sort of person to order thousands of men to walk to their deaths on barbed wire and into a veritable storm of bullets. But neither side was in short supply of those special men.

You tilted your biplane and looked pityingly down on the trenches. You could see the shell-bursts and the wave of men advancing on the German trenches. You could hear nothing over the racket of your engine, but many of the figures beneath you had stopped moving and you knew full well why.

Even for you in the Royal Flying Corps this war was

becoming intolerable. Your comrades were gaunt and hollow-eyed from stress and lack of sleep, added to which was the knowledge that they could very well take off at dawn and never be heard of again. The 'planes were not all that reliable either – patch-up jobs from previous battles and tended by mechanics quite as tired as the pilots. More than once you had made a harrowing return as your engine developed a fault. All you could do was carry on and hope that there would be an end to it one day.

This was what threatened you now, because there was a glinting in the sky ahead and you were being approached by three German aircraft. They were also of the fast variety, which you were not. You heeled over and headed back, running for cover, as ordered.

But there was no outrunning them. They were coming up fast behind you. Your chances were growing slighter by the minute. You leaned forward and yanked back the bolts of your two machine-guns. This finally looked as though it might be your turn.

Since you could not outrun them there was only one thing for you to do. You turned back and headed straight for them. It might well be that they would send you down, but you had every intention of taking at least one of them with you.

As you expected, they split, one peeling off to the left, one to the right and the other coming in head-on. It was an old trick, and you had seen it often enough before. One took you on while the others waited for an opportunity to take you from the side or the rear.

But you were not going to accept that. You decided on the one to the left, flipped your 'plane over and raced in at it. As you had hoped, he had been relying upon your inexperience, and experience was one thing in which you were not lacking. There were enough lines on your young face to bear that out.

And there he was, totally unprepared and lined up directly in your sights. You had outfoxed him. Without hesitation, you squeeezed both triggers and poured bullets into him.

10

The pilot reared up in his cockpit and oil belched from his engine. He was finished.

Immediately you straightened your craft then drove it up into a climb. But you were not good enough. Bullets tore into your 'plane from behind – and then some found you. Your mission was over.

Bad luck on that one.
To find out what might have happened go to **17**.

11

You saw the sailor's gaze fixed on the axe in your hands, his expression one of horror. It was obvious that he was going to try to stop you, and you had no intention of letting that happen. Without even a glance at your companions you hefted the axe above your head and brought it crashing down onto the nearest jar. The sailor shouted with fear and rushed back out through the door. You heard him spinning the sealing mechanism behind him.

'What have you done?' Peri cried.

'Smashed the jar,' you said, already knowing you had acted foolishly. 'The Doctor wanted to examine the plants. Now he can.'

Her face was ashen. 'You idiot!'

Your confidence had already faded. You shrugged the knowledge away. 'There was nothing else to do.'

'And that?' the Doctor asked quietly.

You looked again at the shattered fragments of the jar. The plant was already feeling its way out. It looked dangerous, threatening.

A voice came from a speaker above your head. 'You in there, this is the Commander speaking. What have you done?'

'I've smashed one of the jars,' you said.

There was a pause, then, 'Is the plant still alive?'

'Very much so,' the Doctor said, eyeing the emerging menace.

11

There was a note of resignation in the voice now. 'We shall let you out. Whatever you do, don't stay there.'

Moments later the door was unfastened and you rushed out, to find yourselves confronted by the Commander, his face set, his lips tight. 'Why did you let the plant free?' he asked coldly.

'We wanted to see what it was,' you explained nervously.

'Then I shall tell you,' the Commander said. 'It is called Leechen. It is the only plant our Space allies, the Tandars, can eat. At the moment the Tandars are holding our enemies at bay, but they are running out of food. You have now destroyed our only chance of getting it to them.'

'W-why?' you stuttered.

'Because once the Leechen is freed from the jars it will grow and grow until there is nothing left for it to feed on. Then it will suffocate. That will take approximately twelve hours, Earth time. Once dead, it is useless as food. It decomposes.' He turned away, barely able to contain himself, then turned back. This time his voice was murderous. 'What you have done is to guarantee that the Tandars will be defeated, then Earth will be invaded. All we have done you've turned into nothing.'

You certainly lost that time. It was a result of acting too impulsively.

Try again on **4**.

12

The Doctor's wondering mind was too much of an influence on you. . .

You were alone in the capsule. All the instruments were checked and showing ready for blast-off. As chief test astronaut you had gone over them minutely. Single Personal Orbital Reconnaisance (SPOR) were keen on this mission, as you well knew. Too many computer-controlled vessels had gone astray. What was needed was the human brain to see where the malfunction lay. It was up to you to find it.

'One minute,' the Controller warned.

'Ready,' you answered. 'All systems OK.'

Then came the countdown, and you made one last study of the instruments arrayed before you. All was well. You braced yourself for the send-off from the space shuttle. That had held its station for three years now and had proved itself worthy in all respects, not only in gathering information but as a jumping-off point for more distant voyages. Yours was the problem machine. All the principles were known and understood, yet still there remained that undetected fault. Well, doubtless you would find it. That was your job.

The shuttle's ram-jets blasted and you were jammed back against your seat as they hurled you into Space.

'A-OK,' Control said. You're on-course this end. How is yours?'

'Good,' you replied. 'All readings in order. All going well.'

Far beneath you the Earth lazily turned, blue, green and patched with the white of clouds. It was still startlingly beautiful in your eyes, though you had seen it from this vantage-point many times before. Now you were passing over the Australian continent and could clearly see the burnt brown of the arid interior. It was still a mystery to you how the Aboriginals survived in such surroundings, but nature is a wonderful thing and Man was born to adapt.

As you had adapted to your life in Space. Not everyone could do it. Not too many could adjust to the infinite solitude of traversing the heavens. Insanity had too often been the result.

But that was not for you. Calmly you surveyed the instruments, then realized that one had gone to red. 'I'm off-course,' you said to Control. 'There's no sign of the indicator being faulty.'

'We read you,' Control replied. 'We're trying to correct from this end.'

'Then you'd best be quick. The way I'm going I'll sail right out of orbit.'

'Checking.'

'How long will it take?'

'A matter of minutes, that's all.'

That's all, you thought drily to yourself. If this could not be corrected you were in a tight spot. Not that you were in any way panicked; you had encountered many a problem before. That was the essence of being a test-astronaut. Nonetheless, the element of doubt crept in, as it always did. You were paid to take risks; it was your profession. But always the nervous system took over and the adrenalin started to flow through the veins.

'Control here. We can find no fault this end.'

'None showing here, either,' you said. 'So what is it?'

'Not known. Still checking.'

A thought struck you. 'Have you checked the ram-jets? There might be a fault there.'

'Will do now. Wait.'

You waited, alone and drifting in the SPOR, and aware of the excited urgency all would be undergoing back on the shuttle. Computers would be clicking away, messages flashing onto screens, memory tapes whirling this way and that. All your trust was placed in the experts back there and you knew they were worthy of it. Not for nothing were they in charge of the project. Compared with them you were a mere cipher.

Eventually Control came back to you. 'Fault located. You were right. It's in the ram-jets. It seems that, on firing, they went a fraction of a degree out.'

'Seems?' you said. 'Either they did or they didn't.'

'They did.'

'So?'

'We'll send help as soon as we can. Good luck.'

But would it be in time, you wondered. Everything told you that you were moving further out of orbit by the minute. Within hours you would be moving away from Earth, and as far as you could see, all hope of rescue. You had enough supplies for three months. And then?

Your story ends there.

You would have been better served by **28**.

13

The vat tilted out even further, and a panic-stricken Peri made to leap away. But her effort was in vain. Unseen hands gripped her and held her there. No matter how she struggled, there was no escape. She could feel the numerous hands forcing her to remain in place.

The vat tilted even further, and she could see steam beginning to release itself from the loosening top. She screamed for help, but there was no one to hear.

Knowing nothing of this, the Doctor stood to one side with Burrigan in the control room. 'I trust you're watching your men,' he murmured.

'I always do,' Burrigan said. 'That's my job.'

'Then I suggest you keep doing it. Some of them are looking mutinous. There could be trouble.'

'Doctor,' Burrigan said, 'if you look carefully at me you will notice that I carry a revolver at my side.'

The Doctor accepted the sardonic tone of Burrigan's voice. 'It would be difficult not to notice it.'

'Well, it's there for a purpose. There are many strains in Outer-Space work and sometimes people give way beneath it. The first one to do so now will be shot – by me.'

'I just thought I'd mention the fact.'

'And I thank you. Perhaps now you'd let me know why you don't seem to be afraid.'

'Ah.' The Doctor waved the question aside. 'I've too much to interest me. There's no time for fear.' He smiled. 'Panic, yes. Fear, no.'

Burrigan returned the smile. 'I doubt I'll ever see either in you. You look to me like a born survivor.'

'But with all the human foibles – sometimes more than most. Nonetheless, I'd keep an eye on the men if I were you.'

'I take your point.' He glanced at his watch. 'Your young friend seems to be taking a long time to prepare the coffee. That would help calm them down.'

'I'll go and see what she's about,' the Doctor said.

But at that moment the speakers came into life. '*Aran* calling *Medusa*. Come in please.'

'*Medusa* here,' Burrigan replied. 'Are you all right, Commander?'

'Right as rain. Don't know what happened there. Some sort of interference, I suppose.'

'It sounded as though you were in trouble.'

'Not so, I assure you.'

Burrigan still had his doubts. 'I'll have you up on video, if you don't mind.'

'By all means. Proceed.'

Burrigan nodded to the operator, who flicked several switches. Onto one of the screens came a picture of Commander Wingfield. A cheerful face was his, looking as though nothing could shake the character behind it. 'Am I clear?'

'You are.'

'And you're satisfied that all's well?'

'Yes.'

'Good. We're still making all speed and will contact you again soon. Out.'

They saw Wingfield move away from the screen and the operator flicked off the video. 'I wonder what could have caused that interference?' Burrigan said to the Doctor.

'I wonder,' the Doctor echoed quietly. 'I'll go and see what Peri's up to.'

What Peri was up to was getting dangerously close to an extremely nasty end. She was gasping with fear. The vat was nearly over now, its contents only a matter of millimetres from the tilting lip. Still her struggles were in vain. Still the unseen hands held her where she most definitely did not want to be. Her eyes bulged with terror.

The Doctor came in, took in her plight at a glance and leapt forward, knowing that whatever was holding her must have a corporeal form in order to do so. His outstretched hands touched something, grasped and viciously wrenched. There was a shrilling noise of pain, but he was not to be stopped. In his fury his hands became like lightning calipers, grabbing he knew not what and flailing this way and that. His rage and haste knew no bounds. Whatever it was he was attacking he cared not what damage he did to it. There was no time for finesse. His friend was in danger, and that was something he could not tolerate. He snatched, he tore, finding a strength he didn't know he possessed.

Then he grasped her about the waist and gave a mighty heave. They staggered across the galley and came to a crashing halt against the bulkhead, both totally out of breath and both staring at the vat. The last bolt sprang free. The vat tilted outwards and its boiling contents cascaded onto the deck in exactly the place where Peri had been held.

'I'd have been scalded to death,' she gasped.

'You would indeed,' the Doctor panted, still trying to recover from his unwonted exertions. 'You couldn't have been closer, could you?'

'But what was holding me?'

The Doctor surveyed the steam clouding the galley. 'I'm not sure.' He took her elbow. 'I think we ought to get out of here. Can you manage?'

'Yes, of course. But I haven't thanked you for saving me.'

'I suppose I should have left you there? Come on; this is not a good place to be.' They made their way out.

You knew nothing of this. You were moving forward with Jackson towards the emergency-steering system. But he tripped and went sprawling. He sat up and rubbed his shoulder which had come into painful contact with the deck. 'What the devil was that?' he wanted to know.

There was nothing you could see. 'I've no idea.' You moved forward to help him.

'Loose objects are not permitted in a spaceship,' he complained.

He was wrong. A lever wrenched itself from the bulkhead and came hurtling toward you. It was only quick reflexes that saved you. It missed your head by no more than a fraction and clattered into a corner. 'Keep down,' you shouted. 'It's starting again.'

It did. But this time you were in a more confined space, and the flying objects were much more difficult to avoid. And this time they were heavier. Jackson was quite unable to rise and you were buffeted painfully this way and that. It was complete bedlam. Jackson shouted with pain and passed out, an enormous gash across his forehead.

You struggled to go to his aid, but you might as well have tried to make your way through a sandstorm of flying boulders, whipped up by a storm beyond human comprehension. It was mere moments before you, too, received a stunning blow to the head and fell into unconsciousness.

The Doctor, meanwhile, had helped Peri back to the control room where he recounted what had happened. Burrigan listened in stony silence, only glancing at Peri to make sure she was all right. Things were getting beyond him. Here he was in command of a ship which refused to be controlled, a dilemma not of his own making. What was he supposed to do? Deep as they were in Outer Space, there was no escape. Yet he had a mission, and it was not within his nature to go back on it. He had risen to his present position from the lowest of the low, as was the practice then. In doing so he had developed a will of iron and a philosophy which did not admit defeat. Yet here he was, confronted with a situation which bore all the hallmarks of exactly that. For once in his life he did not know what to do. Yet the responsibilities of command forbade him from revealing that knowledge to anyone. The slightest sign of weakness or uncertainty could be the beginning of any manner of trouble.

He rounded on Tedder. 'How's our course, Mister?'

Tedder looked at the helmsman's read-out. 'Still varying, sir.'

'And the pressure in the hold?'

'The same, sir.'

'Then keep trying to get both back to normal.'

There was a silence. Tedder looked at the crew members about him, then back to his Commander. 'There is one thing I've noticed.'

'And what's that, Mister?'

'For as long as you try to hold this ship on the course you want we get all this trouble.'

'So?'

'So why don't we stop trying? That way we can find out what's required by whatever it is and be left in peace.'

There were murmurs of assent from most of the crew. They'd had enough, both of the situation and their Commander. They feared they were close to death and could see no good reason for it.

Burrigan's eyes were bleak. 'Are you suggesting that I surrender my command to what looks to be a bunch of poltergeists?'

'I'm suggesting, sir, that we can't fight what we can't see.'

'Then I've got some information for you, Mister.' And this time he managed to make the obligatory 'Mister' sound like a term of contempt. 'I command this ship and I make all the decisions concerning it. Your opinion is usually one to which I pay a lot of attention. But this time your opinion isn't worth the breath you've wasted on it. We go on, Mister. The Venus colony is depending on us and beside theirs our troubles are nothing. Do I make myself clear?'

Tedder bit his lip and replied slowly, 'Yes, sir.'

'Then get the men about their duties.'

Tedder obeyed, though clearly unhappy. Burrigan moved across to the Doctor. 'From what you say, you're a man of some experience, Doctor.'

'You could say that, yes.'

'Then what d'you make of all this?'

'Only that the few times I've encountered it, the ships

concerned have never been heard of again. I say that for your ears only. It's not the sort of thing I'd tell your men.'

'Please don't. I intend us to get through. It's a question of maintaining morale. Your news would not help.'

At that moment you staggered in, bruised and shaken, having left Jackson for dead. You were not seeing clearly, your head spinning from the several blows it had received, but you could vaguely make out the figures about you. Peri rushed to your side, to help you to a seat and you explained, as best you could, what had happened. Your news was greeted with silence. After all, what more could anyone say? Who, in fact, could know which of them would be the next to go? The prospect was a fearsome one.

But Tedder was nearing the edge of doubting his own senses. 'I've read a thing or two about poltergeists,' he said.

'We don't want to hear it, Mister,' Burrigan said.

'But we should,' Tedder persisted. 'The literature on it is quite extensive. And the burden of it is that poltergeists nearly always arrive through the person of a female.' He was addressing the crew as much as he was Burrigan. 'Now to the best of my knowledge there's only one female on board this ship and no one has the faintest idea where she came from. But I notice that everything was fine until she appeared.'

'Are you accusing me of causing all this?' Peri demanded angrily.

'I'm simply passing on what I've read,' Tedder replied carefully.

'You're insane,' the Doctor observed. 'I said this ship has been invaded and I meant it.'

'But by what?' Tedder demanded. 'By something she's brought with her?'

'I'm not listening to this nonsense,' Peri snapped. 'The Doctor's right. You're deranged.'

'Oh, it's quite normal,' the Doctor said cheerfully. 'Whenever there's trouble it's only human nature to seek a scapegoat.'

13

'And I'm not going to be it,' Peri said heatedly. 'I'm not standing here listening to rubbish like this.'

'No, you aren't,' Burrigan said icily. 'I suggest you take your friend to the sick-bay and tend to his wounds.' He turned to Tedder. 'And you, Mister, will keep your idiot theories to yourself. I do not permit anyone to be insulted in my presence, and least of all on my ship. Now get about your duties or, as God is my witness, you'll rue this day for a long time to come.'

Tedder avoided his Commander's gaze, but nonetheless did as he had been ordered. Peri carefully helped you to your feet and led you out to the sick-bay. There she seated you, located the first-aid box and took out ointments and sticking-plasters. She was moving back to you when they were torn from her grasp and hurled across the cabin. She stared dazedly at you, then went to retrieve them. No sooner had she done so than the same happened again.

The situation was hopeless. Whatever it was had no intention of permitting you to be treated. Not that it mattered too much, for your head had cleared by then and your few wounds were nothing to bother you seriously, except for your head, still throbbing from where the missile had knocked you out. 'Leave it, Peri,' you said. 'It doesn't matter now.'

'It does to me,' she said. 'I think I'm going mad.'

'Not you,' you said. 'You're always too much in control of yourself.'

'Perhaps not so much at the moment. It's just possible that Lieutenant Tedder was right and I have been taken over by poltergeists or something like them.'

This was not like Peri at all, and you had no intention of standing by while she lost her spirit. You got to your feet. 'Nonsense. These incidents have happened in places you've never been and to people you can't even claim to know. It all started when that meteorite hit us. Were you to blame for that?' She shrugged hopelessly. 'Right. Then let's get back.'

13

When you reached the control room the atmosphere was tense. 'I said you will keep trying to hold to our course, Mister,' Burrigan was saying.

'And I'm telling you that for as long as we do that this trouble will continue,' Tedder argued. 'The only sensible thing to do is give up.'

'That's not in my nature.'

'It isn't in mine either. But I don't believe in going to the stake against the inevitable.'

You noticed that Tedder was deliberately not using the obligatory 'sir' in addressing his commanding officer. That was not a good omen. Nor did the fact that most of the crew had grouped themselves behind Tedder do anything other than fill you with foreboding. The Doctor, meanwhile, was staring at Tedder as though reading his mind, which he probably was.

'I would have thought that at a time like this, discipline and unity were vital,' he observed.

Tedder rounded on him. 'Would you really?' he asked. 'A sort of "united we stand, divided we fall" approach, is it? Well, it occurs to me that you yourself might be just as big a Jonas as Burrigan here. With two of you aboard it seems to me we don't stand a lot of chance.'

'Whatever you say,' the Doctor said indifferently.

'And I'd remind you that I'm your Commander and will be addressed as such,' Burrigan said.

Tedder glanced about to make sure the crew were with him. You could see that they were. He returned his attention to Burrigan. 'Not any more, you aren't.'

'Do you know what you're saying, Mister?'

'Yes, I do, and I'm sorry about it. But I consider you to be so stubborn you're no longer fit to be in command. I therefore formally request you to relinquish your office.'

Burrigan was rigid with offended fury. 'This is mutiny.'

'So it is.'

'I'll have you court-martialled and clapped in irons for the rest of your life.'

13

'Oh, I doubt it.' Tedder produced a pistol from his pocket and pointed it at the Commander. 'This says that I'm in command now. And when we get back to Earth the crew will back me in my statement that you've taken leave of your senses. That's assuming that you ever get back, of course. There's lots of room in Space for your body to stray about unnoticed.'

It's option time again.
You can decide that enough is enough and join with Tedder.
Or you might decide that this is the sort of behaviour you can't tolerate and hurl yourself at him.
Or it might be that you opt for wisdom being the better part of valour and wait for the Doctor's lead.
If you decide on the first, go to **15**.
The second will take you to **19**.
The third choice leads you to **3**.

14

You pulled your wits together. 'It smells of evil.'

'It certainly does,' the Doctor agreed. 'It is, after all, the home of total evil. It carries the spirit of its owners.'

'It's only a piece of metal,' Burrigan said.

The Doctor raised his eyebrows. 'And a house is only made of bricks and mortar. Have you never walked into an empty one and felt totally unwelcome?'

'I have,' Peri said. 'It's an odd feeling, as though the house doesn't want you inside it.'

'Well, what do we do about this thing?' Burrigan wanted to know, indicating the sphere.

'Nothing,' the Doctor replied. 'Watch.' He moved closer to the sphere, reached out his hand and touched it. Immediately it was gone. He passed his hand through the space where it had been standing as though performing some trick, then stepped back. The sphere promptly reappeared. 'It's got a safety-device rigged. Only its owners are allowed to touch.'

'But where did it go ?' you wondered.

'Probably outside until I'd moved away.'

'Amazing,' Peri said. She sliced a tendril that was getting too close. 'But the Leechen's closing in again.'

It was. Burrigan had been right. The speed of its growth was incredible, reaching ever outward towards you.

The Commander eyed it with distaste. 'This almost certainly means the end for my ship. It's the worst possible thing that could have happened. We're doomed.'

In the control room things were going no better. The Imps were still taking their pleasure in plaguing everyone, to the point where it was difficult for the men even to attempt what they were ordered to do. But still they were goaded to their posts.

The *Aran* came through clearly on the radio. '*Aran* here. Have you tracked and am closing. Over.'

Tedder leapt for the microphone, determined to warn the *Aran* off. But it was a hopeless endeavour. In the flash of a second Imps had appeared all about him and he was beaten brutally to the deck.

'You were warned,' Todd said. 'Don't try it again.' He crossed to the console and surveyed the instruments. He found what he wanted and spoke to the *Aran*.'We have you on the screen, *Aran*. We'll prepare to receive you.'

'Thank you. Normal docking procedure, I take it?'

'All as usual. Out.'

He turned from the console and smiled widely at everyone. 'Well, we'll soon have more company. Won't that be nice?' No one spoke. 'Swing out the grapples,' he ordered and the bullied men hastened to obey, going to their places for the docking routine. But there was a cry of horror as one of them opened his control panel and a Leechen creeper lashed out from it, nearly catching him. He jumped away and shouted a warning. But there was no need; others had already found the same. There were cries of horror and disgust as the Leechen crept inwards from every nook and cranny. The men shrank from the threat, but were again ordered to continue their work. They had no option. Constantly tormented as they were, they had to carry on.

Several tried to protest, but were promptly punished. It was Tedder who called a halt to them with a sharp order, but it was also Tedder who muttered to the man working beside him that perhaps the *Aran* might be their only hope, so best they help her alongside. The message whispered its way through the crew, so they did as they were ordered, trying to fend off the oncoming Leechen as they did so.

Then the *Aran* was hovering alongside. The grapples whined out and she drew gently in with short bursts of her navigating burners. A welcome sight she was, too; their only chance of survival.

She drifted in, then she came onto the grapples with a soft bump. Within her lay the future.

Within the hold you had all decided that you had no choice but to surrender yourselves to Tedder and his mutineers. You had no idea what had happened up front, but you did know that the hold would soon be uninhabitable. The Leechen pressed ever closer, almost sobbing for you, wicked of intent but compelled to eat.

It was Peri who brought you up with a jolt. 'Where's the Doctor?' she asked. 'Where's the Commander?'

You were tempted to comment acidly that the Doctor had probably gone off on one of his exploratory tours when you saw what had sharpened her tone. 'We're cut off,' you gasped, seeing how the Leechen had grown and cornered you both.

'But where did they go?'

'Probably to find out what else we could do, rather than surrender.'

'Maybe,' Peri said grimly. 'But just for the moment, I can see only one course for us to take.'

You nodded your understanding and both of you hefted your machetes and waded in at the growth.

14

Your time and efforts were wasted. There was no defeating it now. As fast as you cut, it grew even more quickly. Soon you were confronted with a solid wall of the seething menace. It was a terrifying experience as you were both forced to retreat before something that multiplied in defiance of destructive blades. You both called out for the Doctor and Commander, but there was no answer.

What you did not see was that two of the dead men had appeared behind you. Each carried a club and each used it, felling both Peri and you at the same time.

You fought for your consciousness, but. . .

Time for a test, this time anagrams.
Here are three sentences with all the letters jumbled.
If you work out 'A' first, go to **8**.
'B' first takes you to **16**.
'C' first takes you to **23**.
Answers are on the last page of this book.
A. OYU DAN RUYO SENDIRF REA ODRABA A CESHPIPAS.
B. NETISNEI SI ETH MEAN FO A TAGRE TENSISCIT.
C. TRIFS TOIN CEAPS WEER HET SANSISUR NI IHTER NUTKIPS.

15

The crew moved forward, and one of them removed Burrigan's gun from its holster. All he could do was stand there in complete impotence as his ship was taken into the control of what was, to all intents and purposes, a rabble. For your part, you were by no means sure Tedder wasn't right. He made sense. And how could you fight what could not be seen? Why not go along with it and see what materialized? It had to be better than being destroyed by you knew not what, in a cause of which you knew nothing.

'I'm with you,' you said.

15

Your companions said nothing, though their looks spoke volumes. Burrigan simply held out his wrists and said, 'Best lock me away, Tedder, because if I get these round your throat you'll never smile again.' He paused a moment. 'Unless it be with that frozen smile one sees upon the faces of so many corpses.'

Tedder looked uneasy for a moment, then nodded to two of the crew who, guns pointed before them, led Burrigan, Peri and the Doctor away to the lock-up. You remained where you were. Tedder stood over you. 'You're on probation,' he said. 'One false move and I shall see to it that you're gone.'

'There won't be one,' you said. 'All I want is your word that my friends won't be harmed.'

'You have it,' Tedder said, then turned to the helmsman. 'Let her ride,' he said. 'Wherever she wants to go, let her go there.'

'Aye, sir.' The helmsman released the wheel and punched the computer to non-operational. 'Steering free now, sir.'

'Very well.' Tedder watched the course-readings fret their way up through the digits, almost as though they were timing a race, except that in this case they were racing through fractions to full degrees. 'I thought so,' he said. 'We're going somewhere.' He turned to his men. 'But I don't yet know where.'

They didn't seem to care. It was nice not to have their lives threatened by murderously flying objects. You felt the same. You had a guarantee of the safety of your companions, and this seemed the most sensible course. Tedder was not a man to be trifled with, and who was to say that his judgement was any more awry than that of Burrigan? There were times when you had to work things out for yourself, and this was one of them. Occasionally Peri and the Doctor needed more caring for than you did. This was such a time.

The ship veered a little, then settled on a course. All anyone could do was await the outcome. You knew whence you came, but knew not where you were going. Until a planet hove into sight.

'Planet ahead, sir,' the helmsman said. 'Course eighteen, three four five point four two. Boosters set for landing, planes out, reversing for set-down.'

'Let it be,' Tedder said. 'They're controlling the ship.' He confronted his men. 'I don't know where we're going, gentlemen, but someone seems to need our presence. You will have noticed that since we gave way we've had no trouble. Does anyone have an argument?'

No one did. The men studied him gravely. Peace might bring a price, but then they were prepared to wait and see what it was. Not that you all had to wait long to find out. The ship inverted itself and the rockets went into retro. You landed in a green place. There were flora and fauna, but no people to be seen. The reason for this soon became obvious. The inhabitants were invisible. Oh, they were there all right; you knew this because they spoke to you. At first it was a strange experience, because voices came literally over your shoulder, yet you could see nothing. But they were friendly. My word, they were friendly. They explained how it was that they came to be as they were. They had physical strength, but little ability to manipulate objects. There were distinct limits to their physical abilities. It was easy for mankind to cope with spanners and the like, but for them it was nigh impossible. How to do it? They had brought you here to find out. Being invisible was no fun. It imposed limitations. How do you cope with technology when you have more or less half an arm?

But you were wined and dined. You slept in glorious comfort. You all strolled along the beaches in the mornings, swam if you chose, swanned through each day as though it were of your own making – and yet so little was asked of you. Even Peri, Burrigan and the Doctor took to the life. Dear me, a rest had been a long time coming, and here it was. Paradise enough, sufficient unto the day thereof.

15

All that was required of you by your invisible hosts was a couple of hours a day dismantling your ship. Then you were required to reassemble it. This was no tiresome task. It gave you all something to do before your afternoon siesta. There is little to criticize in a couple of hours of simple tasks, followed by a light lunch, a couple of hours with the eyes closed, and the rest of the day to yourself. There is a lot to be said for it.

But the crunch came, and too soon for your liking. It happened that in reassembling the ship, the drive had been removed. Without it, you were marooned, as soon became all too obvious. Your invisible hosts kindly explained to you that all your operations had been to one end: they could not use their manipulative abilities sufficiently well, so they had studied yours in the disassembling and reassembling of the ship. They had learnt a lot.

But not quite enough. They were still confronted with the problem of constructing corporeal bodies, so that life and the practice of technology became even easier. To this end you were all to become the subjects of scientific investigation which, the human organism being as complex as it is, would take some considerable time.

Well, there was no alternative; time would have to be permitted to pass, then liberty would come, you thought. But the disillusion came, and with a nasty jolt, at that. The investigation, it seemed, was to be surgical. Every one of you would, in turn, go under the knife. Your future, such as it was, was to be a human guinea-pig. What was to be left of you by the end was anyone's guess, but it was not difficult to work out.

That was a poor option.
To find what might have happened, go to **3**.

16

You returned to consciousness in a warmly furnished room. It was obviously designed for the comfort of humans. But that definitely did not apply to the thing standing beside you. It was a robot, built in approximate likeness of human beings; that is, it had a head and arms, though in place of feet it had wheels. A small orange light gleamed on its forehead, doubtless to show it was activated.

'Are you well, Controller?' it asked.

You stood up. 'Controller?'

'We obey the commands of all human beings. Unfortunately, you are the only one left to us.'

'What happened to the others?'

'They were captured by the Xeron, who also cannot function for long without humans. They invaded at night and disabled us. Then they took away our masters. Without them we shall soon lose our will to exist. That will be the end.'

'What happened to their own masters?'

'The Xeron developed wills of their own and were due to be eliminated. Before that could happen they wiped out their humans.'

'Because they were becoming dangerous.'

'That is the case. We are hoping that you will help us to return our masters to us.'

'Me? What can I do? I mean, you look pretty powerful to me. If the Xeron are the same I don't stand a chance.'

'They are the same, except for what has happened to their mind-circuits. But humans are more nimble than any of us and think more quickly. If you will try to rescue our masters we shall provide you with armament.'

You thought for a moment. It was clear that this robot meant you no harm, in fact it was asking for your help, whereas the Xeron sounded dangerous. Robots with minds of their own were capable of anything, not least taking control of their masters and enslaving them, which would mean the end of this particular civilization for your fellow-beings, something you could not allow. Yet the prospect of taking on machines as strong as these was a daunting one. The one before you, for instance, was as hefty a piece of machinery as you would ever wish not to be confronted by. But a cry for help was something you could not ignore.

'You'd better show me the weapon, then,' you said, 'and give me directions.'

'Thank you, master.'

You were led to another room, this one colder in decor, a functional area with rank upon rank of machinery lining the walls. Other robots moved this way and that, going about their duties, programmed to do so despite the absence of their Controllers. They looked towards you but carried on.

Your robot reached onto a shelf and took from it what looked very much like a pocket-calculator. But that it was not. It was a disintegrator, and you were shown the keying of it, the measured tones of your guide taking you through it again and again until you understood thoroughly. Then a map came up on a screen and you learnt the location of the captives. The route was easy. Getting there promised to be something of a problem.

'It is now night-time,' the robot finally said. 'It is a good time to go, master.'

You set off, carefully staying away from the roadways which were all the machines could move upon. Several pickets were stationed here and there along the way, but none sensed you as you skulked through the darkness, the weapon ready in your hand. But there came a point where you could no longer hold to the fields; only the roadway remained. And no sooner had you set foot upon it than three robots came bearing menacingly down upon you, their forehead-lights beaming in the night. They had sensed you and meant business.

There was nothing for it but to see if your weapon would do as you had been told. You pointed it at the group, offered up a brief, silent prayer. As instructed, you keyed it in, for all the world as though you were looking for the answer to a mathematical problem. What you got was somewhat different. It gave off a faint crackling sound and, before your astonished gaze, your opponents burst into blazing red heat and were gone. Whoever had created that particular piece of technology had known what he was about. It was no wonder the Xeron had taken such trouble to surprise the humans. Any warning would have seen them wiped out.

Repeatedly you had such encounters and again and again the weapon wiped out the opposition. You came to the compound housing the captives and freed them. There were no more than thirty of them, but enough to run the city they inhabited. In a tight group you retreated to your starting-point, where the robots showed their pleaure by trundling this way and that about their returned masters.

All seemed to be well and you wondered how to leave, since you had completed your mission and felt it was time to be on your way. But the leader of the humans, Roland, having thanked you on all their behalf, then asked you to stay to help them.

'How can I help you now?' you wanted to know. 'You're free. All you have to do is make sure of your defences.'

He shook his head. 'I'm afraid it's not that simple. You see, over the centuries we've grown so used to the robots doing everything for us that we've lost the ability to think constructively. More precisely, we have no knowledge of strategy. You obviously have, or you wouldn't have been able to save us.'

'That was only common sense,' you said.

'To you, certainly, but not to us. We are now confronted with the problem of either altering the brain-circuits of the Xeron or destroying them. In either case we shall need a mentality which functions like yours, either to capture or attack, not to mention strategically defend. Please stay and help us. We shall be eternally grateful.'

You looked about you at the faces watching you with such hope. They were your physical brethren and their future was problematical. How could you leave them to almost certain defeat and slavery? You would never be able to live with your conscience.

16

'OK,' you said. 'I'll do what I can.'

Their faces lit up and you were glad of your decision.

And so you should be. That was a noble gesture. But it nonetheless ends your story.

Probably things would have been different had you gone to **23**.

17

Clipped to the bulkhead was a row of murderous-looking machetes. You jumped forward, snatched one free, and went slashing in at the Leechen. The Imp merely watched, smiling as you fought the battle in which you had no option. Peri and the Doctor came in to help.

The Leechen sighed and even cried but, oddly, your efforts seemed to be making no impression. In fact, on the contrary, it seemed to be multiplying before your eyes. It was.

'You're wasting your time,' Burrigan called. 'It'll grow more quickly than you can chop it back.'

You turned to him in mystification. 'That's not possible, is it?'

'It is with Leechen,' he said. 'The more you attack it, the faster it grows. You're only hastening the end.'

'But we can't stand here helpless,' Peri protested.

'You have no choice. Eventually it'll cover the entire ship.'

You looked in puzzlement towards the Doctor. He only shrugged, pretty well as puzzled as you were. This was something even he had not encountered before. You had to accept that the Commander had no reason to lie about such a thing. That being the case, you were as helpless as Peri had said.

The Imp giggled and vanished, where or how you had no idea. Burrigan stood in silent impotence. The Doctor ambled off and you, for your part, did the best you could for the slashes on Peri's face. Deep they were, and unlikely to stop bleeding for some time. She accepted the handkerchief you gave her and held it pressed to them, her eyes wide with fright.

The Leechen continued to reach out for you, its growth visibly faster than it had been initially.

In the control room the Imps and dead men had now taken complete charge of the crew. While the dead men gave the orders, the Imps plagued the crew, prodding them with their weapons, which had turned out to have power-packs and caused considerable pain when brought into contact with human flesh. They giggled away among themselves and clearly enjoyed the distress they were causing. Being controlled by both the morbid and the malicious was more than Tedder and his men could take. The very concept made the flesh creep, never mind the actuality of it. But what were they to do? They had supported the First Lieutenant in taking over the ship and now it had been taken from them. They were sliding through deep Space in a ship controlled by ghouls and maniacs. What was to become of them they had not the remotest idea.

In the hold the Doctor had returned to you. 'I need some help,' he said.

'To do what, Doctor?' Burrigan asked.

'To pursue a theory. These Imps can't have jumped through Space without a vessel of some sort. There has to be a craft. I'd like to find it.'

'And how do we do that?'

'By chopping through until we find something. If all four of us go at it we should get somewhere.'

Peri and you knew the Doctor sufficiently well to abide by his suggestions, however whimsical they might seem. Burrigan, too, saw nothing to object to in the proposal, so you all hacked your way in the direction he indicated.

It was hot work, and you were all soon wiping the sweat from your foreheads. But you kept at it, even though, as often as not, the Leechen seemed to be getting the edge on you. The strange mewling and sigh-sound it made as your blades cut into it was far from pleasant. And always and ever it was reaching out for you, seeking the sustenance it yearned for. You didn't fancy letting it find it.

At last the Doctor's theory was proved right. There before you was a metallically gleaming cylinder, some two metres in diameter.

'As I thought,' the Doctor said.

You all wanted to know. It looked like a craft of some sort, you had to admit that, but what sort precisely? And where had it come from? You were full of questions.

'Those Imp things,' the Doctor expanded. 'They travel through Space in this vessel, then transmute into anything they come across which takes their fancy – in this case, us.'

'But why?' Peri demanded.

The Doctor pondered a moment. 'Parasites upon life itself, as far as I can gather. Pure evil is something it's impossible to explain. Disruption and misery would be the aim, I imagine, ends in themselves, needing no justification – at least, not for beings like the Imps.'

You had difficulty in grasping this. 'You mean they have no morals whatsoever?'

'Not in any sense we understand. The best way to look at it is to think of a black hole, which is negative energy. *Negative*, please note, not simply an absence of it. So anything we consider good, they would consider bad. And the reverse. That's the best explanation I can give.'

Burrigan was baffled. 'And they can materialize wherever they wish?'

'Mmh.' The Doctor nodded. 'First they did so in the meteorite, then they headed for you and did the same.'

Burrigan stared in disbelief. 'You mean, that thing came through the hull of my ship as though it didn't exist?'

'Precisely.'

You all stared at the sphere, at the same time giving an occasional chop to keep the Leechen at bay. There was an aura about it, something totally inexplicable. It held your

17

gaze and you felt something happening to your mind, a slipping away from reality, the beginning of a pleasant lack of focus in your sense of logic. You warmly wondered, wrapped as you were in the influence pulsating from it, whether it could take you elsewhere, as it did the Imps, in time as well as space?

Now it's time for another game of chance, to pit your luck against that of the others.
Take three pieces of paper. On one, print 'A', on another 'B' and on the last 'C'. Fold them so that you can't see which is which and drop them into any box, tin or hat.
Take out one of them and unfold it. If you have drawn 'A', go to **25**.
Should it be 'B', go to **27**.
If 'C', go to **14**.

18

You volunteered to help the repair crew. Burrigan and Tedder looked at you doubtfully, and you pointed out that you could carry tools with the best. Burrigan conceded the point, knowing that he needed all the men available, and ordered that you be kitted out with a Space suit. And a strange experience it was. The suit itself was quite light, as was the helmet, but the boots were magnetized and required considerable effort to lift them and step forward.

You were paired off with one of the crew, Davis. He gave you some welding equipment to carry and you and the repairmen crowded into the air lock. The air was drawn out and when the indicator showed zero pressure the outer door was opened. You experienced a moment of vertigo as the awesome sight of empty Space, blacker than you had ever seen and punctuated only by the distant stars, seemed to draw you outwards. Following the others, you stumped your way out and made your way heavily after Davis.

'Stick with me,' he said into his helmet radio. 'Just give me the tools as I ask for them and take 'em back when I've finished.'

'Right,' you said.

His helmet turned towards you. 'Did you hear me?'

'Of course,' you answered. 'I'll do as you say.'

'I can see your lips movin' but I hear nothing. Try it again.'

'Testing,' you said, a little concerned now. 'One, two, three, four. . . .'

'No good,' Davis said. 'Yours is a spare suit. Prob'ly 'asn't been checked properly. Your radio's packed in. Never mind. When I point, just give me what I want.'

But you did mind. It was one thing to be able to hear, but quite another that no one could hear you. Still, there was nothing to be done about it. The work had to be done, and reasonably quickly at that. Holding your lifeline as well as the tools, you plodded after Davis as the others spread out and went about their separate chores. Walking in more or less complete nothingness was a new experience for you, and you had to admit there was something unnerving about it. But Davis was unperturbed and you drew courage from that.

He located the fractured seam and crouched over it. It looked to be bigger than had been thought and his voice was concerned. 'That thing caught us quite a wallop. This is no five-minute job, mate, believe me. Five hours, more like. And not easy to get at, either.'

He took the welding torch from you and set to, the flame burning out into the vacuum, obviously designed for the purpose. The others, you noticed, were examining the rest of the hull for possible further damage and one party was prising away the meteorite with huge crowbars. All were busy, all intent upon their work, Davis particularly, wordless as the flame of his torch liquefied then sealed the damaged seam.

The trouble was that after more than an hour you grew bored. The wonder of Outer Space began to pall. There ought to be something more useful you could do than stand there holding the craftsman's spare tools. You were interested to see just how far the damage led. You decided to look.

Crouching down, you put your hands against the ship's side and pushed your boots away. You knew this to be safe because you were travelling at the same speed and anyway the life-line was in your hand. You pushed yourself below and beyond the absorbed Davis to look further. It was as you had thought: the fracture ran some two metres beyond where he was working. It was going to be a longer job than even he had thought. You decided you had better convey the bad news to him.

You pushed yourself away again to return to your starting-point. It was then that panic struck. You saw Davis hold his torch to one side as he examined the work so far accomplished. He did not know you were suspended in Space, your only security the life-line. Nor did he know that his torch was burning through your only security.

'Davis!' you screamed, but, of course, he could not hear you.

The torch severed the line. You drifted. You screamed and tried somehow to swim your way back to safety. You kicked and shouted, but no one saw and no one heard, all absorbed in their work. In trying to return you had pushed yourself too hard, creating a velocity of your own different to that of the ship. Already you were twenty-five metres away, with no link to your haven.

You were sweating with fear. Your screams were unheard and therefore unheeded. The *Medusa* dwindled against the vastness of eternal Space. The stars sparkled on in total indifference. You sank away into the darkness, the vast solitude creeping chillingly into your soul. There was nothing but you, drifting alone into infinity.

You didn't do too well on that one. It pays not to take chances when you aren't sure what you are about.
Try again by going to **9**.

19

None of this was to your liking. You hurled yourself at Tedder, but yours was a vain attempt. The crew were too quick for you and you were floored before you could get anywhere near him, as was Burrigan. The four of you were herded into a corner and two crew members stood guard over you. Burrigan was helpless and Tedder now in charge.

'Let the ship go where it will,' he ordered the helmsman, who did as ordered.

'And where d'you think that might be?' Burrigan asked.

'We'll find out, won't we?' Tedder replied. 'But I'm sure we'll have no trouble of the sort we've been experiencing up to now.'

'Only perhaps of a different sort,' the Doctor said.

'You, sir, will remain silent,' Tedder said, feeling the weight of his authority now.

'By all means,' the Doctor replied, eyeing the course read-out.

You did the same. The ship veered a little, then settled on a course quite different from the one you had been steering. This it held. It was going somewhere definite; there was no question of that. The only question was: where?

It was not long before you found out. To your astonishment, an entire fleet of spaceships hove into view. There must have been some twenty of them, and their common feature was that they all had gun-ports. This was no merchant fleet peacefully transporting goods from one planet to another. The intention here was fairly clear. But you wondered what the armament would be used against.

The fleet assembled about the *Medusa* and one came in alongside, to connect itself to the *Medusa*'s entry lock. Within a short time a group of men came inboard, all wearing black uniforms and all armed. Their leader looked about him. 'Who's in charge here?'

'I am,' Tedder said. 'First Lieutenant Tedder.'

The leader switched his gaze to Burrigan. 'And why isn't he?'

19

'I refused to let the ship be steered by someone else,' Burrigan replied. 'And this looks to me very much like a hijack.'

'No, no,' the leader said calmly. 'We have a slight difficulty with the planet Timbor. That is to say, we're at war with them. We need all the ships we can get. That's why we drew yours in. I trust we didn't cause too much chaos.'

'You did worry us,' Tedder said.

The leader was unconcerned. 'It was necessary.' His manner became brisk. 'This ship is to be armed and will join us in battle against the Timbors. I trust we can rely upon your co-operation?'

Tedder nodded. 'Of course. My men will give you all the help they can.'

'That had better be plenty. I want gun-ports cut and armaments mounted. How many of your crew have had battle-training?'

Several of Tedder's men raised their hands. 'That'll be enough,' the leader said. 'Right, let's get to it. First the cutting and arming, then we'll have more fuel transferred to you so that you can manoeuvre as necessary.' He pointed to you. 'That one looks fit enough. Lend a hand, you. We need all we can get.'

You had no choice but to obey. The work was done as required, the cutting in such a way that no air leaked out. In no time the *Medusa* was a battleship. Burrigan queried the safety of the Leechen, but was curtly reminded that if the ship received a direct hit there was no way the Leechen could survive because there would be no oxygen to support it. It occured to you that there would be none to support you either, but you were in no position to complain.

The fleet assembled in formation, gave a brief burn-off in unison, then rocketed towards Timbor. You could not help but admire the precision with which they all held formation. This was no haphazard collection of converted merchant ships. This was a flotilla of professionals – barring you, that

19

is, though there were enough professionals now aboard to make sure you, too, held exact position.

For yourself, you were stationed at a port to assist a gunner called Terrance. A quiet, grim man he was, steely-eyed and monosyllabic in conversation. To any of your questions he mostly either grunted or ignored you altogether.

The enemy came into view and, before you knew it, Space was full of hurtling ships, rockets blasting and guns hurling bolts at each other like forks of lightning. It was a thrilling sight, though a frightening one. Several ships of both sides exploded and drifted helplessly away into Space, probably never to be seen again. Too many bolts came too close to you, as far as you were concerned, but Terrance remained his normal withdrawn self and gave no indication of concern. In fact, he turned out to be a deadly gunner, with a speed of aiming and firing that filled you with awe. He seemed to sense when a target was coming up and was waiting for it. He destroyed two ships that you saw, one exploding completely and hurling debris everywhere, the other limping away from the fray with a gaping hole in its side, its survival in considerable doubt.

Then it was over. What remained of the Timbor fleet surrendered and its crews were taken prisoner. You found yourself transferred to one of the captured vessels and headed for Timbor, where the aim was to create a master-colony and soak the planet of its mineral riches. You were to help in the initial stages, when the *Medusa* would be returned to you and permitted to return to Earth.

This suited you well enough. You were content with the prospect of freedom, however distant, though the leader assured you it would not be long.

But things abruptly took on a different complexion. A bomb was discovered in the engine room. It was set to go off in a matter of minutes, too soon for any help to reach you. Immediately experts were sent to defuse it, but the

19

explosives were rigged so carefully that once one connection was delicately severed, another came to light.

All the captured ships discovered the same devices and all were in the same plight. The commander of the Timbor fleet had so arranged matters that every one of his ships would be scuttled in deep Space. He was not a man to surrender either his vessels or his colony to a hated enemy. He was reminiscent of those heroic men of past centuries who had preferred to destroy their command than have it offered up as a prize to the victor.

The experts carefully sweated their way through the circuits, a snip here, a clip there. The minutes clicked away. The labour continued. You all waited in breathless anticipation.

There was a series of explosions. For a matter of seconds Space was brilliantly illuminated by the total destruction of the captured ships.

Considering that you were aboard one of them, you lost that one.

Why not try again from **3**?

20

You volunteered to join two of the searchers, Davis and Logan, and set off along the corridors. Neither of the men looked particularly happy. Come to that, you didn't suppose you did, either. There was no explanation for anything that had happened. It bore all the semblance of a nightmare. There was absolutely nothing about it to cheer the soul.

'I reckon we ought to turn back to Earth,' Davis said.

'Fat chance,' Logan said. 'Jonas Burrigan'll see us all off before 'e's through.'

'Then he's the only one ready to die,' Davis replied. 'Because I'm sure I'm not.'

'Don't 'ave a lotta choice, do yer?'

'Not with him in charge. And anyway, when I die I want to

have a rough idea of where my body's going to be. It wouldn't please me to think about it vanishing from where it's been put and going God knows where.'

'Me neither. A corpse needs a bit o' security, don't it?'

It seemed to you that the conversation was getting more than a little morbid. Still, you were only a visitor trying to help, and there was nothing you could do except follow.

This you did until you reached a particular cabin and the two men led you into it. And there was a man very much alive. He had a cheery red-cheeked face, twinkling blue eyes and a ginger beard. His clothing was so casual he might well have been taking a stroll along the front at Bondi Beach. You all stopped and stared in disbelief.

'Gidday,' he said. 'Let me introduce myself. The name's Roge.' He grinned. 'Roge by name and rogue by nature. An honest feller y'see. I recognize me own shortcomings, even if they do make me rich.'

'And what are they?' you asked.

'I'm by way of bein' a robber.'

'But what are you doing here?' Davis asked.

'I stowed away, mate. I'm good at that. Practice makes perfect. It's a busy life, dodging those security guards at the spaceports. But there we are; life is full of these little trials.'

'You mean you *want* to go to Venus?' Davis asked incredulously.

'Not exactly. No, you could say that is not the main aim of my life. After all, there are better places to be, aren't there? For meself, I'd rather be deep-sea fishing off the coast of Queensland, and that's where I intend to be pretty soon. Just one planet to visit and it's me for off to the land of sunshine, cricket and fishing. Australia, mates; God's own country.'

'I'm not with you,' Logan said. 'If you're not goin' to Venus, what are you doin' on this ship?'

'I intend to rob it, me old son.'

'Like hell you will,' Davis said. 'You'll be in irons so fast your feet won't touch the ground.' He moved forward threateningly.

'Now, now,' Roge said soothingly. 'Let's not be hasty. Why don't we discuss this matter reasonably? I'll explain the matter to you and you'll make a few bucks out of it. Quite a lot, in fact. Enough to retire on. All you've got to do is listen – for the moment, anyway.'

'I'm listenin',' Logan said. 'We all are. What's a few minutes between friends?'

Neither you nor Davis said anything, so Roge took that as assent. 'It's like this,' he said. 'I know a nice place where Leechen fetches a pretty price – fifty times the market value. Now you work that out, fellers. No, I'll do it for you. It comes to five million universal credits. Not peanuts, is it? I'd reckon it's enough to set up quite a few people for several lives, which is what I've got in mind. After all, the credit's worth fifty Australian bucks, twenty-two pounds Pommy cash, thirty-nine Yankee dollars. Not the sort of cash money to be passed by lightly, is it? Not something you'd tiptoe round. More like something you'd grab with both hands.'

'Where is this "nice place"?' Davis wanted to know.

'Planet Ferula.'

'But that's a planet for bandits.'

'Correct. I've retired there quite often myself. The Law can make life very trying at times. But,' he raised a thoughtful finger, 'it is also barren, me old son. Leechen is its life blood. And because it's bandit space, Leechen is difficult to get in. It's also difficult even to get hold of, because of legal controls on its sale. So a fellar like me makes his own decisions.' His eyes twinkled. 'I've made one. I'll have this lot on board here. Get it for nothing and flog it for five million readies. Neat?'

'But you can't do that,' you protested. 'It's plain robbery.'

'Good on yer,' he answered ironically. 'You've worked it out. For such a young person you've got a good head on you.'

'And we'd get a share?' Davis asked carefully. You could see he was being swayed.

'Enough to guarantee you the high life. Do what you like, go where you please.'

'And 'ow d'you propose to do it?' Logan wanted to know.

'Like this.' Roge reached beneath a bunk and pulled out a metal chest. He unfastened the catch and opened the lid. There, before your eyes, was a cache of guns and ammunition. 'Pretty, aren't they?' he said. 'All that's needed is for us to take over the ship and wait till my own comes alongside. Then we transfer the cargo, make sure this one can't pursue us and we're away. Ferula first, do the deal, split the divi, and back home. We know how to do that without being detected.'

'There's just one thing,' Logan said. ''Ow do we know you won't ditch us once the job's been done?'

'Honour among thieves, me old son,' Roge's face was serious now. 'If I ever did something like that the word would get out and my life wouldn't be worth a split cent. There's a strict code of honour in my fraternity and enough power to enforce it, believe me. They'd put a contract out on me and I'd very likely end up being eaten by the very sharks I want to catch.' He raised an eyebrow in query. 'You on?'

And all three of you were, the thought of such riches being more than any one of you could resist.

It worked out exactly as Roge had planned. The rest of the crew were outraged when you appeared among them with guns. Burrigan's fury knew no bounds. But what could he do? Not a lot of people choose to argue with determined armed men. There is a certain foolhardiness about such an action. Then Roge's ship came alongside and the Leechen were transferred, followed by you.

Roge made the sale on Ferula and you hurtled back to Earth, rich beyond your wildest dreams.

However, there was a snag. The ship landed in a remote section of the Australian outback, but had somehow been

20

tracked and you were greeted by Space police, who were in no mood for either bribe or argument.

At your trial they threw the book at you. You didn't stand a chance, and by the time you were given a life-sentence you were beyond surprise, though it did seem a pity to lose everything and be led away in handcuffs.

But lose you did. Your cupidity got the better of you.
Try again from 5.

21

'May I go with you, sir?' you asked Lieutenant Tedder. 'I'd like to help.'

Tedder looked a query at his commander, who nodded. 'Very well,' he said. 'Follow me.'

He led the way out and you found yourself trailing along one corridor after another until you had no idea where you were. However, you were with the lieutenant, so you had no worries on that score. 'This is a big ship,' you observed.

'Bigger than people think,' Tedder answered over his shoulder. 'She can carry cargo or passengers, sometimes both. At the moment we're only carrying the Leechen. That keeps us light, so we don't even need so much fuel for blast-off, which makes us even lighter and gives us a better head of speed. This ship is versatile, believe me.'

'I can see that,' you said, then returned to the matter in hand. 'What d'you think is happening?'

'I've no idea,' came the answer. 'All I do know is that we'd better find out, and soon at that, or we're in danger of not reaching Venus in time.'

'But aren't you afraid at what's going on?'

'Wrong word. "Concerned" is more applicable.'

There was no answer to that. This man was trained to face anything that occurred, and that was what he was doing. After all, there was no telling what might be encountered in Outer Space. Any shortfall in those to whom it happened would almost certainly result in disaster. Discipline was all, and that included self-discipline.

But now you were utterly lost. 'If you carry passengers, how do *they* find their way about the ship?'

'They don't,' came the terse reply. 'They're put to rest and drip-fed for the entire voyage. It's always the same story, you see – weight. We can't carry the sort of food they'd need, nor can we afford to have them wandering about and getting in our way. We might have to act quickly and that could prove difficult with passengers milling about all over the place. One day we might, but not yet.'

He stopped at a cabin door, opened it and went in. You followed, to find yourself in a large area with row upon row of bunks set in it. You guessed there must have been fifty or sixty of them, resting-places for passengers. It would be just as well that they were unaware of their surroundings, because a goodly number of them would have gone insane with claustrophobia.

But what took both of you aback was the sight of a man seated comfortably at a table. An elegant man he was, dressed in evening attire, complete with bow-tie and dinner-jacket, an elegant black cloak draped about his shoulders. His thin face showed no surprise at your appearance.

'Who the devil are you?' Tedder demanded.

'A good question,' came the reply, 'and so apt.'

'Well?'

'My name is Count Dracula.'

You looked at him in disbelief. 'But you're a fictional character.'

'Comfort yourself as you may,' the man drawled. 'But you're looking at me, aren't you? Don't I seem substantial enough?'

Then he smiled and you saw his fangs, a chilling sight indeed. It was easy suddenly to believe all the tales told about him. The books and films had been right, even down to his oily black hair.

21

'But you belong on Earth,' you said.

'No, no, dear boy,' he answered. 'I did and I admit it freely. But life there was so tiresome, if "life" is the word I'm seeking. Every time the sun came up I had to climb back into my coffin.' He sighed. 'Oh, the sheer boredom of it. Quite intolerable.' He brightened. 'Whereas, out here there is no such thing as a dawn and I'm free to sleep and wake as I please. And there's always nourishment about somewhere.'

'Where?' Tedder asked.

Now his smile became an ugly grin and his fangs more prominent. 'I do believe I'm looking at some right now.'

There was a rustling about you and you jerked round – to find yourself surrounded by attractive women. They all had one thing in common: all were grinning and all had bared fangs. The door through which you had entered was now locked and bolted.

'My travelling-companions,' Dracula murmured. 'I'm afraid there's not enough time to introduce you. Terribly sorry.'

He got to his feet and moved toward you. The women also began to close in. You were surrounded by grins and evil.

For you the story is over.
To discover what might have been go to 5.

22

The directions the Doctor's mind took were sometimes beyond belief. . .

You stood on the platform and glanced down at the sea of faces in the circus below you. Some were looking at you and others at Sheba, the elephant you loved, as she did her balancing-act on the small tub. A beautiful animal she was, and gentle. Every day she would wrap her trunk affectionately about your neck when you paid your regular visit to her.

The trapeze bar was in your hands. On the platform

opposite was Rolando. He, too, would swing out at the same time as you, his job to catch you in mid-air. His eyes were cold and for good reason. He was aware that you knew that he was slowly poisoning the animals. Several had already died painful deaths. His motive was simple: he wanted the opposition circus, Karlins, to have a monopoly. They had offered him a sizeable bribe and he was an inveterate gambler, forever ready to get his hands on any loot that was about. This you had learnt about from a friend. All you lacked was proof. The question in your mind was, how long it would be before he got to Sheba?

You flexed yourself, nodded to Rolando and swung out above the crowd. Three times you went to and fro, gathering the necessary momentum. At exactly the right moment you let go, spun yourself through a triple somersault and reached out for Rolando's hands. He caught you safely and landed you on the platform he had left. The crowd applauded loudly. So far, so good.

But your next act was the really tricky one: it was a mid-air roll, your body rigid as though diving into water, and the timing of the catch had to be immaculate. Had you been Rolando and out to do a mischief this would have been the time to choose. You hoped he wouldn't.

Out you went, to and fro, then into your roll. But by moving your head quickly you kept an eye on Rolando. It was in his eyes that this time he meant to let you go, and that at the most dangerous point; where you could easily miss the safety-net and crash to the ground. You reached out in mid-air and he fluffed it, missing you by a millimetre . But that was enough. For the briefest of moments you hung there, then hurtled earthwards, your chances apparently nil.

But they were not because, without Rolando's knowledge, you had rigged extra safety-nets to the side. You hit them, bounced safely and scrambled off, the audience exhaling in heart-pounding relief. To prove to them that you were unhurt you crossed to Sheba and smoothed her forehead.

22

Her trunk wound warmly about your neck. The audience cheered and you waved your thanks to them.

It was not long before Ron, the circus owner, extracted the truth from Rolando and sacked him on the spot. You were left with the problem of finding a new partner, but at least you were still with Sheba and had no intention of leaving her.

Nor would I. This time the ending is a happy one, but it is still the end for you.

Had you gone to 28 *you could have continued.*

23

When you came to you found that Peri and you had been tightly bound. Two of the dead men had bludgeoned you and an Imp stood beside them. Once it saw that you were both conscious it smiled a malicious smile and cooed an instruction to its assistants, who picked you both up.

'What are you doing?' Peri demanded.

'Just making you a little more comfortable,' the man holding her said. 'We want you to enjoy yourselves.'

They hefted you both to the side and laid you down in dangerous proximity to the Leechen. To your disgust the tendrils began to reach out towards you and you could not move. There was threat enough, but one of the men had to move you in closer and say that he didn't want you to be too far from 'the heat'.

Things did not look good.

While this was happening to you, the *Aran* had locked on and its walkway had been connected. All was expectancy. Help was at hand. Tedder and his men waited. There had to be some way out of this misery. The Imps jumped this way and that. The dead men loitered. All depended upon how the *Aran* could deflect this curse that had descended upon them. The Leechen crept its way ever in, bringing with it the threatening end and consuming the oxygen as it did so. Not that any ship could carry more than was essential, so not only was the threat a physical one but organic as well. Lungs starved of oxygen do not fare too well. Ask any doctor, least of all the Doctor, who would be only too pleased to give you a half-hour lecture upon the various functions of the body, starting from the top of the skull and working his way down to the soles of the feet. Not that any of this would have contributed a smidgeon to the morale of the crew, at its lowest ebb ever. They had had enough, far enough from anywhere as to make no difference and controlled by Imps and dead men, not to mention the oncreeping threat of the Leechen. So much a man can stand, then his mind gives out. These men had about reached the end of their tether.

They waited to see what the *Aran* would present.

In the hold, the Doctor called for you. A wall of tendrils writhed before him and Burrigan. But where were you? Where was Peri? They chopped and hacked at the evil growth but, as before, it was very much a losing battle. The faster they chopped, the faster the growth. There appeared to be no way they could defeat it.

'Why can't we even hear them?' Burrigan asked.

'Because of the Leechen,' the Doctor answered. 'It's created more or less a solid wall between us. No sound will get through that.'

'I don't know why I followed you,' Burrigan complained. 'I thought you were intelligent.'

The Doctor nodded. 'Oh, I am. We'll find them, I think. The question is: how?'

How indeed?

In the control room the door from the *Aran* at last opened. In strode the Commander, pink and cheerful. 'Good-day, all. Everything going well, shipmates?'

'No!' Tedder shouted. 'Get back aboard your ship.'

'Why?'

'We're in trouble – more than you could even think of.'

The *Aran* Commander surveyed him blandly. 'Oh, I wouldn't say that. In fact, I'd go so far as to say you're in more trouble than you think.' He turned to the Imp standing beside Tedder. 'Crew of the *Aran* taken under control. Everything now under your command. I await your orders.'

And everyone's heart sank as more Imps came in through the door from which he had just entered. They looked ever so jolly.

In the hold the Doctor had stilled. Burrigan grew irritable. 'Well, you aren't achieving much, are you? Put that marvellous brain of yours to work, why don't you?'

'I am,' the Doctor replied. 'Do I recall you correctly as saying that Leechen won't grow if deprived of oxygen?'

'You do. So what?'

The Doctor indicated the implements fastened to the bulkhead. 'Are they fire-extinguishers?'

'What the hell d'you think they are – under-arm sprays?'

'Keep your levity for later,' the Doctor said. 'What I want to know is, are they foam for killing fire from lack of oxygen?'

'Burrigan looked briefly perplexed. 'Yes . . .?'

'Then use your head and let's get to work.'

The Doctor snatched one from its clip, punched the cap and started spraying the Leechen. The foam leapt out, tangled with tendrils, then covered them. The Leechen cowered, then folded, no longer able to find the oxygen essential to its breeding. Burrigan quickly saw what the Doctor was about and joined him.

Out went the spray as they used gun after gun. Down went the Leechen. The hold was a firmament of flying globules. Bubbles and clusters filled the air. And all the time the Leechen cried before it went down. But still they gunned their way on, firing before them as though using flame-throwers, but in equally as deadly a manner. As they cleared the path they stepped forward, walking over the silenced plant as though over a carpet.

They found you.

With no ado they freed Peri and you of your bonds and helped you up. Peri gave the Doctor a dour look. 'Travelling with you is begining to lose its charm,' she said.

The Doctor looked at her in what, in any other person, would have been total innocence, but in him was completely unconvincing. 'Why is that?'

'It's too dangerous,' she said, stepping aside from a still-moving tendril. 'With you it's one shambles after another.'

'Oh, surely not,' he said. 'What about that lovely holiday we had on Xanthe?'

'What about it?' she said. 'Ten dawns of peace and quiet, followed by what? Nothing but chaos. I tell you, Doctor, I'm growing tired of it.'

'Surely not,' he said in some indignation. 'Who could wish for a fuller life? Consider what you'll have to look back upon. Won't that be something to tell your grandchildren?'

'A full life?' she said. 'Full of what?' It was not often you saw Peri in this sort of mood, but she was in it now. The threat of the Leechen had got through to her and she was in no temper to pay attention to Burrigan, uneasily watching the sprayed plant beginning to struggle through again. 'And anyway, you assume a lot. What makes you so sure I'll live long enough to even consider what a full life is? The way you carry on, my chances are as close to nil as anyone's can ever be.'

'Now, now,' the Doctor protested.

As they wrangled on, your mind drifted away again. Admittedly, you could only travel through Time and Space with the Doctor and TARDIS, but under the unwitting influence of the Doctor your mind could go anywhere – which is what it proceeded to do.

Well, where is your mind going this time?
Let's see how your maths are.

24

A. In your head, multiply 12 by 16.
B. In your head, divide 160 by 4.
C. What is 1% of 1,600?
If you answer 'A' first, go to **8**.
If it should be 'B', go to **16**.
On the other hand, if you find the answer to 'C' first, go to **28**.
Answers are at the end of the book.

24

The vat of boiling water groaned and creaked menacingly as another holding bolt sheered. Peri stood like a stone, transfixed. Then suddenly the realisation of danger engulfed her like a welling tide. She turned sharply in the confined space of the galley and at that moment the door swung shut. . .

In her terror, Peri could not tell whether the ship's motion had caused it to closed or if some unseen hand of evil had incarcerated her, dooming her to an agonising death. She dragged at the door handle in panic. Nothing happened. She shook the handle, pushed the door and finally, in desperation, hammered against the unyielding mass screaming at the top of her voice. And no one heard. . .

Meanwhile you had followed Lieutenant Jackson into the emergency-steering cabin in the aft of the ship. On the surface everything appeared calm and normal, and with luck – and Jackson's expertise – you would soon have the ship back on course. As you looked around with interest, Jackson peered more closely at the computer screen.

'Hellfire,' he muttered to himself.

Intrigued, you went up and looked over his shoulder.

There was no doubt, something was badly wrong. The heading the *Medusa* was now on was taking her far from Venus and the planet's desperate inhabitants. And even if Jackson were able to correct the course immediately, it would be touch and go as to whether the fuel would hold out.

Tentatively, Jackson set the new co-ordinates. The figures on the screen flickered then held. He tried again but it was no good. Something much stronger than the *Medusa's* computer system was taking over. . .

'Well, there's only one thing for it,' murmured Jackson.

You looked puzzled as he picked up the ship's intercom. 'What's that?' you asked. But he was too intent on trying to get hold of the control room to answer you. From the earpiece all you could hear was crazy static.

'What are they playing at? Everything on this ship's going haywire! Look, you're going to have to go back to the control room with a message. Tell the Commander that the only solution I can see is that we go into manual override. If we make a joint effort from the control room and here with the auxiliary, we might just be able to fight this thing and get back on course. Got that?'

'Ay ay, Lieutenant,' you said, sounding more confident than you felt. You set off back towards the Leechen-hold, leaving Jackson scratching his head in puzzlement and vainly trying to find the cause of the problem.

You ran at full tilt until you came to the Leechen-hold. There you slowed almost to a crawl. The omnivorous plant fronds swayed in your direction, reaching out their hungry tentacles as you sidled past the jars. Though logic told you that the thick, toughened glass would hold them, it didn't stop you feeling like an extra tasty packed lunch.

You were extremely glad to leave the Leechen-hold behind you and as you crept past the last jar you broke into a run. Breathless, you pounded along the gangways and as you approached the control room you heard a muffled thumping. . . Boy, were you out of condition; that must be your own heartbeat!

But no, the knocking was too irregular. Slowing down, you cautiously turned and listened. Someone was definitely pounding on that door over there.

25

Cautious now, you walked slowly to the door and listened carefully. There were so many strange happenings on this ship that maybe if you opened the door you would unleash some untold evil. Anyway, you had to get back to the control room. Every second you wasted the ship was plunging thousands of kilometres into nowhere.

The pounding continued, insistently, unnervingly. There was nothing for it. For good or ill you had to find out what was behind the door. And it could be a real emergency – a matter of life or death.

'Who's there?' you called out. There was a muffled answer from the other side of the door but it was so distorted that you couldn't tell whether the voice was human or alien.

Counting to ten to calm your nerves, you tentatively took hold of the handle and turned it downwards. Nothing happened. Well, maybe it was for the best.

'Don't be a coward,' you told yourself. This time you grabbed the handle and pushed it firmly upwards. There was a click as the latch gave way and the door flew open.

In front of you stood Peri, white-faced with panic. You also saw the last bolt of the water tank sheer away and its boiling, scalding contents came thundering like a waterfall to engulf you both. . .

You were right. It was a matter of life or death – yours. Sorry, you were too late this time. Go back and try again from 5.

25

The sphere drew your mind inward, your eyes closed, and. . .

The guillotine sliced down and another aristocrat went to his maker, head rolling into the basket awaiting it. The crowd in which you stood roared its delight, as did you. The old women seated with their knitting about the base of the blade cackled and crowed with glinting malice in their eyes.

What a day it was in Paris, the people ragged but happy, their odour steaming up towards the heavens, yet convinced that their age of Liberty, Friendship and Equality had at last arrived as yet another tumbril filled with aristocrats rolled into the square, bearing them to their doom. Mostly the aristocrats, both men and women, held their heads high in disdain as the malodorous uprising rollicked about them, but some were not so sturdy, and wept for their lives from those they had so abused.

They were not to retain them. On that day the guillotine was busy and bloody, the crowd in no mood for mercy but bent upon revenge on those they held responsible for their appalling lives. Years of hatred welled up about the aristocrats and their existence vanished as though it had never been.

Finally you tired of the entertainment and made your way back to your duties in the Bastille prison, where it fell to you to keep the aristocrats supplied with sufficient bread and water to keep them alive for long enough to meet their fate in a suitable manner. Not that you envied them either their ends or the filthy, infested quarters in which they were at present housed. Your own life was hard enough without being able to spare sympathy where it would do no good.

You moved from one disgusting area to another, doling out the rations, until you came to that of Baron and Baroness d'Auvergne. They still retained their dignity, but little else, their clothes torn and soiled by the mob, their faces and hands dirty from neglect.

You shoved their food through the bars and laughed at them. 'D'you like our palace, then? Is it good enough for you? Will you be in enough luxury 'till your end comes?'

Neither answered. Neither even looked at you. You could feel their contempt. You gave a mock sigh. 'Well, we do our best for you, God knows. Look at the trouble the cook's gone to, preparing your bread and water. You couldn't wish for better. But there we are: nobody's ever grateful – especially you aristocrats.' You began to move away. 'Never mind, though, you won't have to put up with it much longer. Tomorrow morning, isn't it? Well, if I don't see you before then, enjoy yourselves.'

When you left, neither had stirred so much as an eyelash. They therefore had not seen the scarlet rose you had placed beside their bread. Doubtless they would find it in time, you thought. You hoped.

That night you sat with Jacques, one of the guards. He was a slow, dull man, as thick as two planks and quite unable to notice that while he poured your wine down his gullet you took hardly any. It was not long before his eyes glazed, his head slumped and his mouth sagged open. Not a pretty sight, you thought, as you detached the keys from his belt. His gapped and decaying teeth were enough to turn the strongest of stomachs, let alone the stench of his unwashed body. But there: at least you had not had to club him. Life had its compensations.

You stole into the prison area, flitting from one dark area to another until you reached the cell holding the d'Auvergnes. There, you unlocked the door and looked inside. Both were seated and waiting. 'Come on,' you hissed. 'There isn't much time.'

'Who are you?' the Baron asked.

'Does it matter?'

'Yes. As far as I know, you're a dreadful person who takes pleasure in mocking our plight.'

'Then you don't know enough. I'm the Scarlet Pimpernel.'

'And what sort of name is that?'

'Does it matter? You have a chance of life and freedom. I suggest you take it.' Time was running out. You looked toward the Baroness, who was looking at you with some caution. 'Tell him, madame, please. This is your one chance of escaping the guillotine. I beg you to take it.'

She paused for only the briefest of moments, then rose to

her feet, taking her husband's hand and bringing him up with her. 'Come, my love. We are being offered help. For us, what else is there?' She brought him towards you. 'Lead on.'

Somehow you got them out, though it had always been tricky and you had small doubt it would become even more so. Subdued they came, understanding nothing, but still asking no unnecessary questions as you got them into a coach and four and raced for the coast. The further you went, you lashing the greatest possible speed it was possible to get from the horses, the more you could feel their trust extending out to you.

When you reached the coast you could see the boat waiting and ready to go. You helped them into it and, at the last moment, both turned to thank you.

'But you must tell us who you are,' the Baroness said.

'Indeed,' the Baron added. 'May we not know to whom we owe our lives?'

'The Scarlet Pimpernel,' you said and turned away in haste. There were others to be rescued and time was ever short.

You sped away into the night, the horses thundering before you, on the coast you had just left the Baron and Baroness being taken toward the safe shores of England. So much to be done, so many lives to be saved.

Here your story ends. You cannot surrender your oath to save as many friends as you can from the guillotine.
'They seek him here, they seek him there,
Those Frenchmen seek him everywhere.
Is he in Heaven, is he in Hell,
That damned elusive Pimpernel?' (*Baroness d'Orczy*)
Had you drawn more luckily you would have gone to **14**.

26

As the Leechen began to emerge, so also did a noxious gas. The smell was revolting. You felt giddy. Your senses slipped away from you and you fell to the deck.

You were on the bridge of a galleon, its sails full above you, the water choppy enough to make you pitch slightly. Beside you was your Captain, Burrigan, a telescope to his eye as he studied the ship you were trying to overtake. She, too, was in full sail and endeavouring to make more knots than you, though it did not look as though she was succeeding.

Burrigan was a splendid sight in his Royal Naval uniform the epaulettes gleaming on his shoulders. He lowered the telescope. 'We're catching her, Mister,' he said to you.

You were his First Lieutenant. 'Aye, sir.'

'Are we fully prepared?'

You looked along the length of the ship. The men were at their guns, ball and grapeshot stacked beside them, sweatbands bound about their foreheads. They looked ready for whatever was to come, not such a bunch as you would wish to contend with. From the sternpost the White Ensign bravely fluttered. 'All the men at their stations, sir.'

'Right, Mister. We'll have her in a couple of hours, I should think.'

'If the wind holds.'

'I see no sign of it lessening. She's from the east, which is just what we want.' He studied your quarry. 'We'll have that treasure from her if it's the last thing we do.'

'We can manage that, I'm sure.'

'So am I. Those villains have grown too rich at the expense of too many others.'

'They are about to become exceedingly poor.'

'And dead – quite a number of them.'

He meant that. Pursuit was one thing; hand-to-hand fighting was another. You fingered the hilt of the cutlass at your side and trusted you could do your duty as entrustd to your rank.

'I want some musketry up the masts, Mister.'

You shouted the order and the marines clambered upwards with the agility of monkeys, even encumbered as they were with their arms. You watched them as they lodged themselves securely, then fell to, priming their muskets with powder and shot.

Time passed leadenly. You must have been making a good six knots, but your target was doing only slightly less. Sailing required a great deal of patience. But finally there was only a matter of metres between you and she opened up with her stern cannon. The balls flew through the air and you watched them, judging where they would hit and observing the damage. Fortunately, most of them plunged wide and into the water.

'We'll take her from the wind'ard side,' Burrigan said.

The reasoning was faultless. That way you could take the wind from her sails and bring her as near as could be to a halt. You ordered the helmsman to steer fifteen points to starboard, then met her and held the course.

Their Captain was nervous. He opened up well before you were within range, the shot falling hopelessly before your bows. You could see him and his officers on their bridge. He was black-bearded and bulky, and it occurred to you that, while he was doubtless a brave man, his courage was not matched by his knowledge of gunnery. This could not be said of Burrigan. He stood like a graven image, awaiting his moment, not a trace of fear about him. 'When I give the order, Mister, I want the for'ard six guns to open fire. The rest will hold because the second order will be for a broadside.'

Now the brands were flaming in readiness as the gunners prepared themselves. The men glistened with sweat beneath the baking sun. The powder-monkeys crouched and waited for all hell to break loose.

Which it soon enough did. Already their shot was coming inboard and there was the splintering of timber and the cries of the wounded.

'Fire!' Burrigan shouted.

The forward six guns roared out their rage and recoiled across the deck, to be heaved back by the gunnery crews.

Burrigan had timed it well. You saw the balls smash onto your quarry's deck, men reeling this way and that. Again and again the cannon were reloaded and the flaming brands touched to the powder. And still you edged forward until you were almost directly alongside.

Then there was silence as all readied themselves for the broadside. Burrigan carefully watched the pitching of his ship, unperturbed by the shot smashing inboard and the musketry whistling about you. 'Fire' he cried.

Every gun on the port side bellowed out at the same time. Your ship reeled back from the sheer force of it. The timing had been excellent. The deck of the other ship suddenly became complete carnage. You could see men going down by the dozen. Holes appeared in the bulwarks. The forward mast was shattered, hung a moment, then toppled outboard.

Burrigan was ready now as the guns were heaved back into place. 'Reload. Open up with the musketry.'

There came the rattle of the marines as they raked the deck of the opposing vessel.

'Fire!' from Burrigan, then immediately, 'Out grappling irons. Stand by to board. Take her alongside, Mister.'

You gave the orders, even as your shot was wreaking even more damage on your opponent. The helmsman swung the wheel over and you saw her sails sag as the wind was taken from them. The boarders stood ready and you took up your post on the side, in charge of them. Out went the grappling irons and you hauled the ships together. You had your cutlass firmly in your grasp, then Burrigan snapped the order. ''Way boarders!' and away you all went.

It was indeed a version of hell as you and your men hacked your way into the enemy, as bloody a scene as one was ever likely to see. The air was full of ball-shot, screams and flailing blades.

But the day was won and the few enemy remaining

surrendered. You had no idea how may men you personally had wounded or killed; the mêlée had been too confusing. But as the bodies were hauled away you accepted the surrender and you and Burrigan went below, there to find riches beyond your wildest dreams. There were cases of gold coins and jewellery stacked each upon the other, filling two holds. Clearly, the pirates had been busy, not to mention successful.

Burrigan smiled in satisfaction. 'That was a battle worth fighting, Mister.'

You eyed the wealth before you. 'Well, you don't have to call me that any more, do you?'

'No, we can get back to normal – rid ourselves of these foolish uniforms, then haul down that White Ensign and put our own skull and crossbones back. I'll feel more comfortable then.'

'Me too,' you agreed. 'But you must admit, we've done well pretending to be a Royal Naval ship. We certainly frightened the lives out of this lot.'

'That we did. Now we'd best divide this up between us and the men, get our vessel shipshape, then we'll head for Maracaibo.'

'And live a life of luxury.'

Which you did. For an entire year you lived more comfortably than you ever had in your life before. Then one day Burrigan reappeared. He was bored, he said. He had bought another vessel and intended setting out on the high It didn't take you long to decide in his favour. You, too, had found a life empty of incident more than a little wearing on the patience. The call of the sea and adventure was more than you could withstand. Your future had been determined from the moment you had become a pirate. Thus it would continue.

Your story ends there.
To find what might have been, go to **17**.

27

The sphere drew you into a dream and . . . You watched impatiently as the mechanics raced to repair and replace the wheels of your racing-car. Time was against you. You'd been holding the lead until you'd hit some of the wreckage from an earlier smash. Now the German ace, Hildenbrau, stood every chance of winning, and that with only three laps for you to go. Curse that wreckage.

Your car was a beauty, its lines sleek and blue, but you were not in love with it at that moment. What a thing to happen with victory almost in your grasp. Still the mechanics laboured on.

'Just get the wheels on,' you snapped.

The chief mechanic turned an oil-covered and worried face toward you. 'I don't like the look of the front axle. It's badly out of alignment.'

'OK,' you said, 'so I take a chance.'

He shook his head. 'Not without my permission.'

'Since when did I need that?'

'Since I was put in charge of handling this vehicle.'

'But not in charge of me.'

'You're bound to take my advice. You know the rules. And I'm telling you that this car's in no condition for the track.'

You paused a moment as late runners went roaring by, the sound of their exhausts drowning all speech, then you stared impatiently in the direction of the sun-drenched crowd, 'Get the wheels on,' you snapped as soon as you could make yourself heard. 'Do it now.'

The chief mechanic stared at you a moment, then shrugged and nodded to his assistants. They moved with unbelievable speed, snapping on the wheels and spinning the nuts tight as you pulled on your helmet and lowered your goggles. The jack was wrenched clear and you snapped yourself into the cramped driving seat. As they pushed you out and your engine thundered its challenge Hildenbrau flashed by. He was ahead, though by only a few seconds. You could sense that the crowd had risen to its feet, gripped by the drama of the two of you fighting it out on the burning, rubber-streaked track.

The car was tough to handle, but you fought her forward, your knuckles white with the effort of holding her straight. The fencing was simply a white blur as you slammed along past it. When there were only two laps to go you were right on Hildenbrau's tail and judging how you could pass him. But he was a cunning devil and knew how to block your progress, leaving you no room on the turns and riding well out on the straight stretches.

And on the last lap you saw your chance. He had gone too wide on the bend and left a brief opening for you. You pressed the accelerator the last millimetre and were through.

Briefly you saw him raise his hand in acknowledgement of your feat, but there was no opportunity to reply. The front end of your car was veering badly now. Sweat poured down your body as you struggled to hold it steady.

And now you could see the finishing-line. Foot flat now, you hurtled toward it, scenting victory and already anticipating the joy of holding the cup above your head before the crowd and the cameras.

And a bang came from the front. You'd lost the car. The axle had gone. To your horror, you saw the right-hand wheel racing out at an angle of forty-five degrees. The world whipped about you in total insanity, then you were briefly upside-down as you rocketed in toward the fencing.

Bad luck on that one.
Better luck would have come your way had you drawn **14**, *where you might have survived.*

28

But you wrenched your thoughts back to reality, which was bad enough in itself. 'Well, we're all free, but what do we do now?'

83
42

'We surrender,' the Doctor said.

Peri was startled. 'What? To those demons and dead men?'

'There's nothing else for it,' Burrigan said soberly. 'It's the last thing I want to do but, believe me, the foam will soon dissipate and before you know it this hold will be solid with Leechen.'

'Absolutely right,' the Doctor agreed.

None of you wanted to do it, but what you lacked was an alternative. So you made your way back to the control room, where the Imps awaited you. Behind you the Leechen was already beginning to stir, and in the control room was still creeping its way inwards. All you received was dour looks from the dead men and glee from the Imps, who immediately started plaguing you. It was within you to clout one of them, but you knew that the attempt would be useless. You'd be brought down by a gun should you so much as lift a finger.

The crew knew it too, all giving you but the briefest of glances, then returning to their chores.

'Venus calling,' came from the speaker. 'We can't last much longer now. We've scraped the bottom of the barrel. You're our only hope.'

The *Aran* commander switched on his microphone. 'All set now, Venus. We'll be with you in no time. Just hold out.'

'Thank you, Commander. We'll do our best.'

He turned from the console and towards Tedder. Indicating the Doctor and Burrigan, he said. 'Tie those two up.' This was done. 'Now put them over there,' he said, and they were hauled to the doorway where the Leechen would reach them in no time.

But it was not done so quickly that the Doctor did not have a chance to see the ship's position and course. As Tedder placed him where he had been told he whispered, 'Steer eight degrees to port.'

28

The lieutenant looked at him in some puzzlement, but Burrigan understood. 'Do it, Mister,' he said. 'And lock the controls while you're at it.'

The Imps clustered about the two and cooed their delight as the Leechen reached their legs and wrapped about them. Both men were white of face as their fate became apparent. Soon the growth would reach their hands and finally their faces. They knew what awful thing would happen then as their life was drawn from them.

But you saw Tedder alter course while everyone's attention was elsewhere. You did not know what he was doing, but guessed that it was the Doctor's doing, up to no good again. All you could do was wait. It was bad enough that you were in the power of the Imps, but the thought of the Venus colony also being ruled by them was intolerable.

You saw the Doctor and Burrigan shuddering as the Leechen crawled toward its feast, but as yet there was nothing you could do.

Then suddenly there was a planet directly ahead of the ship and coming closer by the second. Pandemonium broke out and everyone raced for Tedder. But there was nothing they could do. He snatched up an iron bar and smashed it down on the steering-controls. Immediately he was hit by bolts from the Imps' guns and fell writhing to the deck. The *Aran* Commander leapt forward and wrenched at the helm, to no avail. It's locked on,' he shouted. 'We can't change course.' He turned to one of the dead men. 'Get down to the emergency steering,' he commanded. 'Bring the ship about.'

'He'll never get through the Leechen,' Tedder said through teeth gritted against the pain. 'You've lost this one.'

The *Aran* Commander gave him a murderous look, yet the infliction of further pain upon the lieutenant would serve no purpose. You all stared in horror at the screens as the planet hurtled in towards you. The Doctor's reasoning was clear to you; better that you all should die than the people of Venus be enslaved. Peri stood near to you, as brave as ever she was and saying nothing. But you could feel her shuddering with the same fear as possessed you. Death was near.

The Imps grouped themselves against the bulkhead, concerned now with their own safety and no longer interested in the situation of the Doctor and Burrigan. They cooed among themselves – then suddenly were gone. The rats had abandoned the sinking ship.

Briefly you saw the dead men lift their heads, as though returning from a nightmare.

Then you hit.

Except that you didn't. There was a moment of total silence as you all flinched from the inevitable, then you were out and floating free, the screens showing nothing but the distant stars. Disbelief filled the air, then the Doctor grinned at Burrigan. 'We were right, weren't we?'

'You were, Doctor. I only followed along.'

'Don't belittle yourself, Commander.' He looked towards you. 'Are you going to set us free, or just sit and enjoy the show?'

Several of you freed them and cut the Leechen away. 'What happened to the planet?' you wanted to know. 'Where did it go?'

'There wasn't one,' the Doctor said. 'We're in a Space-Warp zone.'

You were still puzzled until Burrigan added, 'Refraction. That planet is actually light years away. What you were seeing was its image.' He crossed to Tedder and helped him to his feet. 'Are you all right, Mister?'

'Yes, thank you, sir. But still guilty of mutiny.'

'Not so,' Burrigan said. 'You made what you thought was the best decision. Now we'll forget it. Let's just get on to Venus.'

Peri looked round from tending to the 'dead' men, who had no idea of what had been happening. They had not been dead, only possessed. 'What about the Leechen? Look, it's everywhere.'

Indeed it was, crawling its menacing way in all directions. The ship would never make it to Venus; the growth would fill it long before arrival.

'I think I can answer that,' the Doctor said. He turned to Burrigan. 'Can you empty this ship of oxygen, Commander?'

'I can. But what do we breathe?'

'You all don Space suits and live inside those. Deprived of oxygen, the Leechen are as good as dead. So you can use the emergency steering and still reach Venus in time. Then you revive the Leechen and all is well. Clear?'

'Of course,' the *Aran* Commander said, also returned to normality. 'And when our breathing tanks need replenishing we can do it from my ship.'

So it was agreed. The Commanders and the crew were full of thanks to the three of you, but the Doctor was impatient to be on his way. There was so much learning to be done, so much more to experience. Led by a group of men lashing a path clear with fire-extinguishers, you made your way back to the TARDIS.

Once inside, you said to the Doctor, 'That was close.'

'Very,' Peri added.

The Doctor operated the controls and once again you set off you knew not where. 'You're both too nervous,' he said. 'You really must learn to put all these things down to experience.'

THE END

ANSWERS

Section 14

A. YOU AND YOUR FRIENDS ARE ABOARD A SPACESHIP.

B. EINSTEIN IS THE NAME OF A GREAT SCIENTIST.

C. FIRST INTO SPACE WERE THE RUSSIANS IN THEIR SPUTNIK.

Section 23

A. 192.

B. 40.

C. 16.